D0180131

Click'd

Click'd

Tamara Ireland Stone

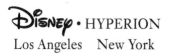 • HYPERION

Los Angeles   New York

Copyright © 2017 by Tamara Ireland Stone

All rights reserved. Published by Disney • Hyperion, an imprint of Disney Book Group. No part of this book may be reproduced or transmitted in any form or by any means, electronic or mechanical, including photocopying, recording, or by any information storage and retrieval system, without written permission from the publisher. For information address Disney • Hyperion, 125 West End Avenue, New York, New York 10023.

First Hardcover Edition, September 2017
First Paperback Edition, January 2019
3 5 7 9 10 8 6 4 2
FAC-020093-19028
Printed in the United States of America

This book is set in Janson MT Pro, Andale Mono MT Pro, Adderville ITC/Monotype; KG Happy/Fontspring
Designed by Phil Caminiti and Mary Claire Cruz

Photographs by CREATISTA/Shutterstock • dicogm/Shutterstock
Rawpixel.com/Shutterstock • tsaplia/Shutterstock • Ohn Mar/Shutterstock
sianc/Shutterstock • Samuel Borges Photography/Shutterstock • Pressmaster/
Shutterstock • dboystudio/Shutterstock • Zurijeta/Shutterstock • William Perugini/
Shutterstock • Bo1982/Shutterstock • PYRAMIS/Shutterstock
ober-art/Shutterstock • robuart/Shutterstock • Alias Ching/Shutterstock

Library of Congress Cataloging-in-Publication Control Number: 2017017706
ISBN 978-1-4847-9924-6

Visit www.DisneyBooks.com

SUSTAINABLE FORESTRY INITIATIVE
Certified Sourcing
www.sfiprogram.org
SFI-00993

THIS LABEL APPLIES TO TEXT STOCK

For my daughter, Lauren.

And for the real Ms. Slade, my sixth-grade teacher, who consistently told the girls in her class that they could do anything *and be* anything. *I'm sure I'm not the only one who believed her.*

Saturday

one

Allie tightened her grip on her phone as she stepped out from behind the curtain and walked to the center of the stage. She looked out into the Fuller University Auditorium. The room was packed with people, and all but three of them were complete strangers.

Speak clearly, she silently reminded herself. *Smile. Relax. Do it exactly the way you've practiced.*

Allie looked down and spotted her parents in the front row. Her mom waved. Her dad gave her a thumbs-up.

Sitting next to her mom was her middle school computer science teacher, Ms. Slade. She had helped Allie get into the highly selective CodeGirls summer camp by working with her on her application, essay, and sample game. Allie smiled at her and mouthed the words *Thank you*. Ms. Slade smiled back as she brought her palms together.

Then the lights dimmed and a spotlight shined down, warm on Allie's skin, blinding her. She was relieved that she could no longer see Ms. Slade. It helped her keep her mind off the real reason her favorite teacher was sitting in the audience.

Allie realized she was fidgeting with her phone, so she tucked it into the back pocket of her jeans and forced herself to stand taller.

She took a deep breath.

And then she began.

"On the first morning here at CodeGirls Camp, our instructor told us we had a whole summer to create any kind of app or game we wanted. *Anything*. Something just for fun. Something that would solve a real-life problem. It was *entirely* up to us. I loved that." Allie leaned forward and brought one hand to the side of her mouth, like she was telling them a big secret. "That hardly ever happens to seventh graders in real life, you know."

The audience laughed.

"But I admit," Allie continued, "on that first morning, I wasn't sure I was ready for that kind of challenge. I was *waaay* too busy being terrified. Because I didn't know a single person."

Allie began pacing the stage. Her legs were shaky and she hoped the audience couldn't tell.

"I kept looking around the room at these girls—nineteen total strangers I'd be spending my whole summer with—and wondering who they were. Did we like the same music? Did we read the same books? Did they have sisters or brothers? Where were they from? I knew we had one thing in common—we were coders—but everything beyond that was a total mystery."

She glanced over to the side of the stage and relaxed a little when she saw her friend Courtney hiding behind the curtain, wearing a huge grin and nodding encouragingly.

Allie returned to the center of the stage. "And that's when the idea hit me. Why not an app that could help you make new friends? You know, something to tell you who you clicked with." As she said the word "clicked," she snapped her fingers.

Allie pulled her phone from her pocket and waved it in the air. "For my summer project, I created a game called *Click'd.*" She loved the name. She thought it was a catchy way to describe what the app did.

The logo zoomed open on the huge projection screen behind her, and Allie glanced over her shoulder. She beamed every time she saw it; she couldn't help herself. She loved the soft blue background and the white, pencil-thin swirls that formed two stick figures with their arms around each other.

"Let me demonstrate how it works. This auditorium seats two hundred and twenty people. I assume most of you don't know each other," she said jokingly, and beyond the glare, she could see people looking around and shaking their heads.

"What if I told you there was one person in this room right now who had more in common with *you* than with anyone else?" Allie held her finger up in front of her. "One person who, statistically speaking, you have more in common with than anyone else. Of course, you could leave this room and never know who that person is, but . . ." Allie leaned forward, resting her hands on her knees, and crinkled her nose. "Wouldn't it be more fun to find out?"

Allie waved her phone in the air. "We're going to use that audience-polling app you installed, so, everyone, please pull out your phones and play along."

That was the cue for the stage crew to raise the houselights. Now she could see the audience much better, which meant she couldn't help glancing down at Ms. Slade again. It looked like she was taking notes, but at least she was smiling.

For her nineteen fellow CodeGirls, the presentation was a celebration of all the hard work they'd done that summer—but for Allie, it was that and more. Ms. Slade was a mentor for Games for Good, an annual teen coding competition run by Spyglass Games. Allie hadn't even considered applying for the contest at first, but once Click'd started getting attention at camp, she thought she might have a shot. She'd already sent Ms. Slade the code, but she had to nail this presentation if she was going to fill the last remaining spot in the competition.

Allie took a deep breath and looked back at the rest of

the audience, scanning the room. "Ready, everyone?" she asked as the screen behind her filled with four scenic photographs. "Which do you prefer: the ocean, the forest, the desert, or the mountains? Select A, B, C, or D."

She advanced the slide.

"Now pick a favorite dessert." The screen displayed four new images: a bowl of ice cream, a slice of cake, a candy bar, and a piece of apple pie.

Allie looked down at her screen. She could see the data collecting in the app she'd built specifically for this demonstration. It used the same algorithm as Click'd, taking all the information the audience entered and immediately matching people with overlapping interests.

"Let's do some more so we have lots of information to work with," Allie said, and she flipped through seven additional slides, asking the audience to pick a favorite superhero, car, breakfast cereal, word, sculpture, color, and houseplant.

"When you're done with the quiz, Click'd figures out how you scored against each person, but it doesn't immediately tell you who your top friends are, because that wouldn't be as fun," she said with a wink. "Instead, Click'd uses sounds, lights, and clues to help you find your top ten friends."

As she walked across the stage, she noticed her legs weren't shaking anymore. She pressed a few more buttons on her phone.

"I'm shortcutting things since this is a demo."

Allie tapped on her screen, and one of the phones in the back of the room let out a sound that startled its owner. "Sir, would you please stand?" She tapped another button, and a phone in the front row on the opposite side of the theater sounded. A woman held her phone in the air and then stood and turned around.

"Congratulations! If you two were playing Click'd, you'd be in a spot on each other's leaderboards." They waved at each other from across the theater.

"That's basically how my game works. You take a quiz, the algorithm figures out who you have the most in common with, and then it uses your smartphone's geolocation capabilities to help you find each other."

Everyone clapped as the man and woman took their seats.

Allie glanced over at Courtney again. She had a huge grin on her face. Allie looked back at the audience, feeling on top of the world.

"The leaderboard is dynamic, constantly changing as new people join."

The screen behind Allie filled with a picture of the CodeGirls, running around the computer lab with their phones high in the air, trying to find their matches.

"As soon as Click'd identifies someone on your leaderboard who's within three hundred feet, your phone flashes blue and it *bloops*." Allie brought the microphone closer to her mouth and whispered, "That's a technical term," and

everyone laughed again. "When the two of you get within one hundred feet, it *bloops* twice and turns yellow, and then, when you get within thirty feet, it turns red and gives you a hint: a photo from that person's Instagram feed."

Allie rooted her feet in place. She was feeling good now. She didn't look at Ms. Slade. She didn't need to.

"When you find each other, you tap your phones together and see where you rank on each other's leaderboards. Then you hear this sound."

Woo-hoo!

The audience laughed again, and Allie couldn't help but smile. "That sound is telling you to take a selfie together. The picture is sent to the whole user community to announce the newest click."

She advanced the slide to a photograph of two CodeGirls with their arms around each other, and then another set of two, and another set of two.

Then she opened Courtney's profile.

"This is Courtney. We landed in the number one spot on each other's leaderboards."

A photo of Allie and Courtney filled the monitor. Then Courtney walked out from behind the curtain and threaded her arm through Allie's.

"Obviously, there's more to friendship than overlapping answers on a quiz. But in our case . . ." Allie and Courtney looked at each other. "An app helped us see how much we had in common." They both snapped their fingers at the same time. "And we clicked."

The two of them bowed and the room exploded with applause. Allie and Courtney waved and ran offstage. Their CodeGirls instructor took their place, thanked Allie, and introduced the next presentation.

When they were behind the curtain and out of sight, Courtney hugged her. "You were amazing!" she said. When she pulled away, she gripped Allie's arms with both hands and looked right into her eyes. "You have nothing to worry about. Your teacher is going to love it!"

"I hope so!" Allie said.

As soon as the presentations were over, Allie saw Ms.

Slade heading up the steps and onto the stage. She reached for Courtney's hand, squeezing it hard, like she could wring good luck out of it. Ms. Slade stopped in front of them and looked at Courtney. "Your game was fantastic!" she said, and Courtney thanked her. Then she looked at Allie.

Allie hadn't seen Ms. Slade since school got out. Now that she was standing so close, she could tell her hair was a lot shorter, and that made it even curlier than it usually was. But otherwise, she looked the same, with her rich brown skin, and her warm, friendly eyes, and as always . . . the earrings.

Allie beamed when she saw her little swirly stick-figure friends on the light blue background. "You made Click'd logo earrings!"

The earrings were Ms. Slade's trademark. She wore different ones every day—pizza slices, tiny power tools, lightbulbs—all made on the computer lab's 3-D printer.

"Of course I did," she said as she batted her fingers against them. "I made a pair for you, too. I thought you might want to wear them onstage next weekend when you present at the Games for Good competition."

Courtney gripped Allie's arm harder.

"Really?" Allie asked.

Ms. Slade nodded. "I've been digging into your code all week and trying to break it, just like the judges will. And I've gotta say, it seems to be rock solid."

Allie looked at Courtney. "The CodeGirls have been

helping me test it all summer. If they can't break it, no one can!"

Ms. Slade was beaming. "And your demo was perfect. The judges are going to love Click'd."

"I told you!" Courtney said.

Allie had built apps before—fun games for her friends and word puzzles for her parents, but she'd never made anything like Click'd. She felt like she was about to burst with pride.

"So let's make it official. What are you doing next Saturday, Ms. Navarro?" Ms. Slade asked.

Allie stood up taller, threw her shoulders back, and put on her game face. "I'll be presenting in front of a thousand people at the Games for Good competition." She tried to stay serious, but she couldn't seem to get her mouth to cooperate.

Ms. Slade gave Allie a fist bump. "Do exactly what you did up there today and you'll knock it out of the park." As she walked away, she called over her shoulder, "Don't change a thing."

Monday

two

Allie rested her lunch tray against her hip and took a deep breath. *Relax,* she told herself. *They're going to love it.*

Her friends were sitting at their usual table out by the big oak tree. When Zoe saw Allie coming, she jumped up from her seat, ran to meet her, and threw her arms around her.

"You weren't on the bus," Zoe said.

"My dad gave me a ride." Before Allie could get the words out, Emma was pushing Zoe out of the way, and Maddie was on her other side, fighting for space, too.

"You're back!" Maddie said.

"When did you get home?" Emma asked.

"Late last night," Allie said. "It took me forever to pack up my dorm room and say good-bye to everyone, and then my parents insisted on taking me to dinner to celebrate."

Her friends knew what that meant.

"You got into Games for Good?" Zoe asked, and Allie nodded fast.

"I knew you would!" Emma said.

"We never doubted it!" Maddie added.

They all walked back to the table together. Allie sat between Zoe and Emma, just like she had all last year, and Zoe gave her a playful bump with her shoulder. "Missed you, nerd."

Allie smiled and bumped her back. "Missed you more."

Then Allie rested her elbows on the table and looked at them. "I can't believe I haven't seen you guys all summer. What did I miss? Tell me everything. Like . . . what was the best soccer tournament?"

"Oregon!" Maddie shouted at the same time Zoe yelled, "Lake Tahoe!"

"No way!" Emma said as she slapped her hand hard on the table. "Are you kidding me? San Diego was the best! Highlight of the summer. No question."

"What are you talking about?" Maddie asked. "It was *insanely* hot . . . like a hundred and two degrees the entire time. We were *melting* on that ridiculous black turf. How could that have been your favorite?"

"One word," Emma said. "Pool." She looked right at Allie. "When we got back to the hotel after the first day, the whole team ran straight for the pool. We kicked off our cleats and jumped into the deep end holding hands, in our uniforms and everything!"

Allie felt a little twinge of jealousy. She'd been so caught up in her own world all summer, she hadn't thought much about what was happening back home. She hadn't missed a soccer tournament since third grade. It was so weird to think that her best friends had more than two months of memories that didn't include her.

"Wait. You're all skipping the most important part," Zoe said.

"What?" Maddie asked.

Zoe threw her arms up in the air. "Waffles?"

Emma let out a sigh. "Oh, brother. Here we go again."

"The breakfast buffet had one of those waffle makers that flips over and cooks two waffles at once." Zoe pulled her hands away from the sides of her head, like it was exploding.

Allie laughed. "What is it with you and those waffle makers?"

"Crispy on the outside, fluffy on the inside. They're magical. Like unicorns. Or . . . Pegasuses," Zoe said.

"Pegasuses?" Emma wondered. "Or Pegasi?"

"I don't know." Zoe tossed a Cheeto at Emma's head and she batted it away. It landed on the table, so she picked it up and chucked it back at Zoe, laughing.

"Anyway," Maddie said. "The point is that we missed you."

"Every day," Zoe said.

Everyone was quiet for a few seconds. Until Emma looked at Zoe and whispered, "But our summer was pretty epic," and she winked at her and said, "It seriously was."

"Come on, don't make her feel bad, you guys," Maddie said. Then she turned to Allie. "Besides, I'm sure coding camp was just as *epic*."

Allie heard the sarcastic emphasis on the last word, but she ignored it. Her summer may not have been filled with hotel pools and tournaments, but it had been its own kind of epic. Plus, the college's cafeteria had one of those waffle makers, too.

"Actually, I had an amazing summer," she said as she unwrapped her sandwich.

Zoe looked at the others, then took the lead and said what Allie figured they were all thinking. "Really?" she asked, drawing out the word. "Computer camp was 'amazing'?"

"Yeah," Allie said. "I mean, I missed you guys every day, but it was even more fun than I expected it to be."

No one said anything, so Allie launched right in.

"We lived on campus, right in the dorms," she began. "It felt like being away at college. And my roommate, Courtney, was super nice. . . . All the other girls were, too." She was talking fast, but she couldn't help it.

"Oh, and I thought the computer lab would be dark and

depressing, but it wasn't at all! It had these massive floor-to-ceiling windows on three sides, so everyone called it the Fishbowl. It was incredible. Superfast machines with giant monitors and a bunch of stations for big animation projects."

Allie thought she might lose their attention completely when she started talking about the Fishbowl, but they still seemed to be listening.

"This is interesting and all," Emma said, "but you've been texting us all summer about this thing you were building." She waved her hand toward her chest in this well-let's-see-it kind of way.

Allie scanned the quad to make sure Mr. Mohr wasn't nearby, then reached into her back pocket for her phone. "I've been dying to show you—"

"No!" Maddie shrieked. She covered her mouth as her eyes grew wide, fixed on something in the distance.

"What?" Zoe asked.

"Hair," Maddie whined from behind her hand as she stared at Chris Kemmerman and his friends, sitting three tables away. "It's . . . it's . . . gone."

Toward the end of sixth grade, Chris Kemmerman seemed to be the only subject that kept Maddie's attention for more than two minutes. Allie had been hoping the novelty had worn off over the summer. Apparently, it hadn't.

"County was two weeks ago," Zoe said matter-of-factly. But she could tell from their blank stares that they weren't making the connection. "All the swimmers shave their heads before the final County meet. It cuts down on drag. Improves their race times." She gestured toward the eighth-grade section on the opposite side of the courtyard. "My brother shaves his arms, his chest. Even his legs."

"He does?" Emma asked, crinkling her nose. They all turned to look at Chris and his friends again, trying to get a better view of their legs.

"Actually," Allie said, "I think he looks even cuter without hair. You can see his eyes now."

"I agree," Zoe said, resting one hand on Maddie's back. "Besides, who needs hair when you have those shoulders? I mean, look at them."

"I guess . . ." Maddie pouted. She let out a loud sigh and said, "But I loved his hair."

Allie scooted her lunch to one side, sat on top of the table, and waved her phone in front of her. "Well, maybe he'll be on your leaderboard."

Maddie's eyebrows pinched together. "What are you talking about?"

Cell phones were strictly prohibited during the school day, so Allie gestured for the three of them to come in closer. They clustered together, knees touching, and leaned in, blocking her phone from view.

She lowered her fingertip to the glass and tapped on the Click'd icon. Her app launched and the words *Ready to click?* appeared in narrow, loopy letters. She felt her chest swell with pride.

"You start by creating a profile with all the typical stuff. Here's mine." Allie tilted the screen toward her friends.

"When you open Click'd for the first time, it asks you about your favorite school subjects, what sports you play, what video games you like, what you look for in a friend . . . that kind of thing. Once it has all the basic data, it goes through fifty items and asks you to pick a favorite. It's like those online quizzes you're always taking, Emma."

"I love those quizzes!"

"I know! I got the idea from you," Allie said, and Emma grinned and tipped her head to one side. "When you're done, it ranks how compatible you are with other people in the system. But here's the fun part—it doesn't show you who they are. You have to find them based on clues."

"Like a scavenger hunt?" Zoe asked.

"Exactly," Allie said.

"So wait," Maddie said, straining over Emma's shoulder to get a better view. "How does it know who's most compatible?"

"It's all about the questions." Allie didn't want to talk in jargon about fields and algorithms, so she answered as simply as she could. "I even made up a fake name and joined a few online dating sites so I could see how they worked. Click'd looks for things two people have in common. That's it, really. The more you overlap, the higher your score. The higher the score, the higher your spot on the leaderboard."

Allie went back to the main screen, tapped on the LEADERBOARD tab, and ran her fingertip slowly down the glass, scrolling through the list of photos. "This is how my fellow CodeGirls and I ranked," she said proudly.

"What's going on here?" Allie looked up in time to see Mr. Mohr standing right behind Emma, trying to see over her shoulder and into the circle. Allie pocketed her phone as quickly as she could.

"Nothing," Zoe said. "Allie was telling us a joke."

The girls scrambled into their seats and reached for their food.

"I didn't see a phone, did I?"

Before Allie could answer, Maddie spun around and looked him right in the eye. "Did you have a nice summer, Mr. Mohr?" she asked sweetly.

Allie could tell he wasn't buying the diversion tactic, but he must have been feeling generous. It was the first day of school, after all.

"It was very nice, thank you," he replied. "My kids and I went to Washington, DC, and New York."

"That sounds so fun!" Maddie said, smiling and nodding, but his face remained completely expressionless.

"It was. I highly recommend it." He locked his hands behind his back. "Welcome back to Mercer," he said, and then he walked away, scanning the quad, looking for his next stop.

Allie waited until he was over by the sixth-grade section, and then she pulled her phone out again. "Wanna try it?"

Zoe, Emma, and Maddie smiled at each other. "Um, yeah!" Zoe said, speaking on behalf of all three of them.

The night before, Allie created a new group called "Mercer Middle" so she could keep her school friends separate from the CodeGirls. She tapped on the pull-down menu and opened it. Allie was the only member, but she wouldn't be for long.

She curled her body over her phone again and navigated to the LET'S CLICK button. It opened her contacts and she selected the boxes next to Zoe, Maddie, and Emma's names. And then she looked at each of them in turn. "Ready?" she asked.

They all nodded.

Allie pressed INVITE.

three

"Let's get out of here," Maddie suggested, and that was all it took for the four of them to ditch what was left of their lunches in the closest trash can and hurry out of the quad, away from the crowds and Mr. Mohr's watchful eyes.

They found a quiet spot on the walkway between the school garden and the science building and sat in a circle, cross-legged and bent over their phones. The three of them took the Click'd quiz while Allie squirmed, fidgeted, and leaned in closer, trying to see their screens.

Zoe let out and a laugh and said, "Okay, that's funny."

Maddie said, "Ha! No way!" as she selected an image.

When Emma kept chuckling under her breath, Allie

couldn't stand it anymore. "You guys are killing me!" she said, and scooted over behind Emma, resting her chin on her shoulder so she could see what question she was on.

"When you see the LET'S GO! button at the bottom of the screen, stop. Don't press it until I tell you to," Allie told the group.

"It wants permission to access my photos and my Instagram account," Zoe said.

"Say yes. It pulls clues from your Instagram feed and stores the ClickPics in your photos file."

"ClickPics?" Emma asked.

Allie grinned. "You'll see."

"Now it wants permission to access my contacts," Maddie said.

"Choose yes again. That's how you'll invite new users," Allie explained.

A minute later, Zoe yelled, "Done!"

"Me too," Maddie said.

"Same!" Emma added.

Allie tapped her toes fast against the cement, feeling giddy as she checked the time.

"Perfect. We have fifteen minutes. Run. Get as far away from one another as possible and tap the button." Allie circled her finger in the air. "And then start walking around campus, looking for each other. Oh, and watch your screen for clues. Blue means you're close. Yellow means you're getting warmer. Red means you're hot. As soon as you find each other, tap your phones together."

"And then what?" Emma asked.

"You'll see," Allie said again.

Emma, Zoe, and Maddie looked at one another, started cracking up, and then took off running in totally different directions, while Allie sat on the cement all alone, staring at the screen and trying to contain herself.

A minute or so later, Allie's phone sounded with a single *bloop* and the screen lit up in bright blue.

She sprang to her feet and ran in the same direction Maddie had gone, stealing glances at her phone and watching for the color to change. The screen was still blue when she rounded the flagpole at the front of the school, but it turned yellow when she ran by the library.

Bloop-bloop.

She ran through the quad, down the steps, past the basketball courts, and turned the corner by the gym.

"Getting warmer," Allie whispered as she glided past the boys' locker room, heading for the staircase. "Who are you?" she asked the screen. "*Where* are you?"

Bloop-bloop-bloop.

Allie stopped cold and looked down at her phone to find a picture of Emma and Zoe with their arms around each other. It was tinted red and flashing, and as she walked toward the staircase, the red screen started flashing even faster.

She took the stairs two at a time, turned the corner, and found Emma sitting on the top step with her phone in the air, displaying an old photo of all four of them, taken at a soccer game.

Allie ran up the stairs as Emma jumped up and down, yelling, "This is so awesome!"

"Now tap," Allie said, holding her phone out to Emma.

"What?" Emma asked.

"Tap your phone against mine."

The second Emma touched the side of her phone to Allie's, both phones vibrated, the red lights stopped flashing, and the photos disappeared. They sat down on the top step and stared at their screens. There was a single flash of white. And their leaderboards opened.

"Number three?" Emma crinkled her nose.

Before Allie could reply, Emma's phone gave a celebratory *woo-hoo* sound and her camera automatically opened.

"Now we take a picture," Allie said. They came in cheek-to-cheek, and Emma held her phone at arm's length. "That's a ClickPic. It goes out to everyone to show off the newest match!"

Bloop-bloop.

Allie's and Emma's phones sounded in tandem and started flashing yellow.

"Someone's close!" Allie held her phone high in the air and Emma copied her.

Bloop-bloop-bloop.

The light on Allie's phone changed to red. Emma's did the same.

"It's Zoe," Emma said, twisting her phone so Allie could see.

"Mine's Maddie!" Allie said.

They heard *bloop-bloop-bloop* from the bottom of the stairs, and a second later, the same sound came from the top. Allie's phone showed a selfie of Maddie in her room, and Emma's phone had a picture of Zoe and her brother at one of his swim meets over the summer.

"They're coming from different directions!" Emma yelled. She barely had the words out before Maddie came racing down the stairs and Zoe came running up.

Emma couldn't stop laughing. Allie was cracking up, too.

"Oh my God, this is so insanely fun," Maddie said, touching her phone to Allie's.

"I know, right?!" Zoe squealed as she and Emma made it official.

Then Allie turned to Zoe and Maddie reached out to Emma. They all held their breath as their leaderboards appeared.

"This is *ah-maze-ing*!" Zoe yelled.

Woo-hoo!

The sound came from all four phones simultaneously. "What's that?" Maddie asked, laughing.

"Now we take a selfie together," Allie said. "It will go out to the whole user community to show that we clicked."

"By 'user community' you mean the four of us?" Zoe drew a circle in the air in front of them.

"Well, for now," Allie said, laughing. "It's just for us until after the competition on Saturday. Then maybe we can invite some more people."

Maddie looked at her phone. "But without more friends, we can't see the rest of the leaderboard," Maddie said. "I just have question marks." She turned the screen toward the other girls. "I can't have question marks."

"Exactly," Zoe said. "We need more users."

"Right? We need everyone in here!" Maddie said as she tapped a manicured fingernail against the glass.

"Like, the whole school," Emma added.

Allie loved how excited they were to share it, but she couldn't let them do that. Not yet. "Just wait till next week, after the competition is done. Then I'll count on you to help me share it with everyone and teach people how to

Click'd — Allie Navarro — Leaderboard
1. Zoe
2. Maddie
3. Emma
4. ?
5. ?
6. ?
7. ?
8. ?
9. ?
10. ?

Click'd — Emma Liu — Leaderboard
1. Zoe
2. Maddie
3. Allie
4. ?
5. ?
6. ?
7. ?
8. ?
9. ?
10. ?

Click'd — Maddie Ellerts — Leaderboard
1. Zoe
2. Allie
3. Emma
4. ?
5. ?
6. ?
7. ?
8. ?
9. ?
10. ?

Click'd — Zoe Jordan — Leaderboard
1. Allie
2. Maddie
3. Emma
4. ?
5. ?
6. ?
7. ?
8. ?
9. ?
10. ?

use it. You can be my street team!" Allie said. But that didn't seem to be what her friends wanted to hear.

"I don't know about that," Maddie said, as she glanced around campus. Allie watched her, thinking that she knew that look on her best friend's face far too well. Maddie was calculating. "You have more than nine hundred kids stuck inside a two-acre campus for eight hours each day. And it's the first week of school, so about three hundred of them are sixth graders who hardly know anyone, along with who knows how many seventh and eighth graders who might want to start off the school year with some new friends."

"What's your point?" Allie asked.

"Isn't your competition all about games for *good*?" Maddie said. "I would think a few stories about it doing *good* on your own middle school campus might be a nice touch, that's all."

Zoe hooked her thumb in Maddie's direction. "She's right, you know."

Allie thought about it. She was dying to see what Click'd could do in the real world. She'd tested it in the lab to be sure it could handle hundreds, even thousands, of concurrent users, and it passed with flying colors. And she loved the idea of sprinkling her presentation with real-life success stories of newfound friendships. But there was too much at stake.

"I can't risk it crashing, you guys . . . not with the Games for Good competition on the line." Allie held up a finger. "Just wait one week. And then it's all yours to share."

31

four

Allie was beaming when she opened the door to the computer lab. She was still thinking about the way her friends squealed with excitement as they tapped their phones together and took their spots on one another's leaderboards. They loved Click'd. She'd spent all summer hoping they would, and they did.

She couldn't wait to get home after school and text her fellow CodeGirls to tell them all about her first real-life beta test. Courtney would be so excited for her. They all would be. She pictured herself on the couch with her dog, Bo, curled up by her side, her fingers buried in his soft fur while she tapped away on her phone's keyboard.

The lab was filling up quickly, and Allie was happy to see that no one had taken the station she'd sat in last year. She was racing toward it when she heard Ms. Slade call her name. Allie turned to see her teacher waving her over. "Can you come here for a second?"

Nathan Frederickson was standing there, too. Allie felt her eyes narrowing as she walked toward him.

She and Nathan had gone to the same elementary school. They were both in the same computer class. Every year, they entered the same contests and competed against each other in the science fair, and Nathan beat Allie out every time. And every time, he couldn't wait to rub her nose in it.

Allie could count her enemies on one hand. In fact, she could count them on one finger. And his name was Nathan Frederickson.

He was wearing loose, light-washed jeans, black slip-on Vans, and a white T-shirt with a big Poké Ball on it. He was taller than he was last year, but other than that, he looked pretty much the same, with freckles spread across his cheeks, and messy red hair.

"Hey," Allie said.

"Hey," Nathan mumbled back.

Ms. Slade must have been able to feel the tension because she laughed and said, "Well, now that we've got those pesky formalities out of the way!"

No smile from Nathan.

No smile from Allie.

"I wanted to congratulate both of you in person." Ms. Slade looked at the two of them. "I can't begin to tell you how excited I am to show off my two Games for Good contestants."

"What?" Allie asked. Ms. Slade hadn't mentioned anything about mentoring Nathan, too. She couldn't be serious. Allie looked over at Nathan and saw the color drain from his face.

"Allie's in G4G?" he asked.

"Yep. I added her last weekend. Wait until you see her game, Nathan. It's extraordinary." And then she turned to Allie. "And the game Nathan's been working on all summer is going to blow your mind!" She drummed her hands on her desk excitedly.

Allie didn't say a word.

Nathan didn't say anything, either.

They were both trying as hard as they could not to look at each other.

"Now, as your mentor," she said, "it's my job to help you get ready for Saturday in every way I can. Your games are solid at this point, so the best thing I can do is to prepare you to wow those judges. And I had an idea on my way to school this morning! What do you think about demonstrating your apps to your classmates today?"

Allie didn't say a word. Neither did Nathan.

Ms. Slade batted at her dangly earrings, showing off her yellow strong-arm emojis. "Remember these? They're my first-day-of-school earrings. They're supposed to remind you to be brave and strong when you walk in these doors every day for the next ten months."

Allie didn't feel brave or strong. She felt nervous. Her palms were getting clammy, so she rubbed them against her jeans. "I would, but I don't have the voting app."

"You can improvise, can't you?" Ms. Slade asked.

"I guess. But I . . . just . . ." Allie heard herself stammering. "I just didn't plan to show it to anyone other than my three best friends until after the competition."

Nathan looked over and raised an eyebrow, silently questioning her, and Allie suddenly felt defensive. She glared back at him. "Not because the code isn't solid, Nathan. It is. It's *rock* solid."

"I'm sure it is," Nathan said with a shrug. But he didn't sound like he meant it.

Allie ignored him. "It's solid," she told Ms. Slade. "It's just that the competition is only five days away and I don't want to jinx anything, that's all."

Ms. Slade smiled at her. "I totally get it, but it's only a demo. You're not inviting your whole advanced computer science class to download it or anything."

Allie nodded. She knew Ms. Slade was right. But still, the idea of showing Click'd to her classmates made her ridiculously nervous; even more nervous than she was onstage back at CodeGirls camp.

Nathan combed his hand through his hair. "Well, I don't know about her, but I'm ready to go."

Allie squared her shoulders and looked right at him.

"So am I," she said, faking confidence more than feeling it.

"Great!" Ms. Slade clapped her hands together once. "I'll do my usual first-day-of-school thing and then turn the show over to you two. Who wants to go first?"

"I'll go," they both said at the same time.

Ms. Slade reached into her drawer and pulled out a quarter. "Heads, Allie goes first. Tails, Nathan goes first." She flipped it in the air and it landed with a *thunk*, spinning in small circles on her desk before it settled on tails. "Looks like you're up first, Nathan."

Nathan shot Allie a smug look and Allie glared at him.

When she turned to take a seat at her station, someone else was already sitting there, and Allie had to take the only desk that was still unclaimed. It was in the first row, right in front of Ms. Slade, and nowhere near the window. She couldn't help but blame Nathan for that, too.

The bell rang. Ms. Slade stood silently at the front of the room, waiting for the chatter to stop. Eventually, when the room was quiet, she began speaking.

"Welcome back, everyone!" she said. "Did you all have an incredible summer?" Some people slouched lower in their seats, while others sat up a little taller. "I want to hear all about it. Who wants to start?"

A few hands shot up, and Ms. Slade spent the next ten minutes going around the room. Brandon told the class about his trip to Hawaii, Kari talked about spending most days at the skate park, and Justin talked about all the books he'd read. And when everyone was done, Ms. Slade told everyone how she spent two weeks in India visiting family and attending her favorite cousin's wedding. She invited everyone to come into the lab during lunch that week if they wanted to see her pictures.

Allie was only half listening. She was thinking about her demo, visualizing how she'd do it without the voting app, and trying to ignore the butterflies that felt like they'd taken over her stomach.

Ms. Slade leaned back on the edge of her desk. "I'll tell you about our new semester project, but first, I have some exciting news to share. Before I began teaching, I spent ten years as a developer at Spyglass Games. While I was there, I helped start the Games for Good competition, a contest exclusively for teen coders, and after I left the company, I stayed on as a mentor. Now each year, I get to bring one talented young developer into this contest. But this year, I convinced the judges to let me bring *two* students: Nathan Frederickson and Allie Navarro. As seventh graders, they'll be the two youngest players to ever enter G4G. Today, they're going to show you the games that got them there. Let's give them a big hand."

Everyone clapped as she waved Nathan to the front of the room. He paired his laptop with the giant monitor and a colorful icon of a house appeared in the center. A second later, two animated characters emerged from the sides of the screen, wearing overalls and shuffling toward the center carrying armfuls of letters. When they reached the house, the two characters threw the letters into the air.

They looked up, watching them tumble around in the sky before settling on top of the house and forming the roof with the name BUILT.

"My Games for Good entry is a fun, interactive game where players work together to build homes—animated ones, and real ones, too."

Nathan clicked on the icon, and suddenly there was a whole neighborhood, complete with streets, sidewalks, trees, and even a tiny playground off in the corner. Dotting the sidewalks were small, cartoonish-looking houses.

"The objective of the game is to build houses." Nathan pointed to the screen, and Allie watched an animated woman in a blue sweatshirt and a white cap, standing on a ladder and hammering on the roof. "Each player starts off with some wood, basic tools, and a few supplies, like nails and plaster. But your original materials will only get you so far. When you run out, you have to buy more at the hardware store." He pointed to a building on the corner. The little characters were running inside empty-handed and leaving with tools, boards, and cans of paint.

"You buy supplies using the points you earn, and you earn points by helping your neighbors."

Nathan left-clicked on a character wearing a red sweatshirt and right-clicked on a house on the opposite side of the street. The little man climbed down from the ladder, tucked it under his arm, and carried it over to the target house. When he reached it, he propped the ladder against the side, climbed again, and began hammering next to another man wearing a blue sweatshirt.

Allie couldn't get over the amount of detail in each character—different skin tones and hair colors, different clothes and hats. Aside from the way they moved across the screen, everything about them was designed to be unique.

She fixed her gaze on the tiny figure with a hammer in his hand and watched the house go up slowly, plank by plank. It started coming together faster once there were two characters working on it.

"Fun, right? But here's where it becomes a game that also does *good*." He zoomed out so the class could see the neighborhood from a bird's-eye view. "It's all about these signs."

Allie hadn't noticed them before, but now she saw the empty street signs and billboards scattered throughout the neighborhood.

"All the signs are reserved for corporate sponsors." Nathan zoomed in on one and pointed at the logo. "I'm sure you all recognize this?"

Allie rolled her eyes. Of course they did. It was one of the most recognized logos on the Internet.

"Spyglass Games," someone in the back yelled.

"That's right. Spyglass isn't an official Built sponsor," he said as he locked his eyes on Allie, "but *when* I win, they will be."

Allie folded her arms across her chest. The class let out an "Oh!" and Allie heard someone say, "Burn!"

"Every time a player completes a house, one of the sponsors donates a dollar to Habitat for Humanity. Since I began developing this game, I've built more than a thousand of these little houses." Nathan was wearing a huge smile now, waving his hands as he talked, and Allie could hear the excitement in his voice. "If I had just one sponsor, we would have raised one thousand dollars. Which would be great, but imagine if we had hundreds or thousands of players, and twenty or thirty big corporate sponsors, each taking turns to kick in a buck every time a player finished a house. That's real money, going to a real cause." He closed his laptop and the monitor went dark. "So that's Built. A real-life game for good."

Allie felt her mouth turn up at the corners. But then she remembered he was her competition and adjusted her expression.

As the room erupted into applause, Nathan bowed exaggeratedly and returned to his seat in the back of the room. He didn't even look at Allie as he walked past her.

"Okay, Allie," Ms. Slade said. "You're up."

Her hands started shaking and her heart started racing. She stepped to the spot in the front of the room and looked around at her classmates.

You got this, she thought. *Don't let Nathan intimidate you.*

As she paired her phone with the wireless projection system, Ms. Slade told the class about the CodeGirls summer camp, and how Allie had been one of twenty middle school girls selected out of nearly a thousand applicants from across the country. Then Ms. Slade killed the lights.

Allie took a big breath. "Take a look around this room," she said. "This is Advanced Computer Science. We've all been in class together for a year now. And we all know that every one of us has one thing in common: we love coding.

"But have you ever wondered what else we have in common?" She pointed to a girl in the front row. "Maybe Shonna and I both love reading. Maybe we even love the same books." She pointed at two boys in the back row. "And maybe Jason and Theo both like horror movies." She pointed at the door. "And what about the people out there?"

She interlaced her hands behind her back. "There are a little over nine hundred students here at Mercer Middle School. You're never going to meet all of them. Not here. Not even when we all get to high school. But there is one person at Mercer who has more in common with you than anyone else." She held up her finger. "One person. What if you graduate never knowing who that person is, simply because you never had a class together? What if you never meet simply because your paths never cross?"

Allie locked eyes with a few people in the room. They looked intrigued.

"What if I told you there was an app to help you find that person?"

Allie realized her hands were no longer trembling. She had the attention of everyone in the room and it felt good.

She tapped the icon on her phone and the Click'd logo

appeared on the monitor behind her. She didn't want to use her newest group since there were only four users, so she opened the CodeGirls group instead. Allie slid her finger down the screen and scrolled through their photos. Seeing their faces made her miss them all over again.

"You start by creating a profile," she said. "For the sake of the demo, let's make our class a person. What should we call ourselves?"

Her classmates looked at one another. Finally, Kylie Rodriguez shouted, "I've got it!" from the last row, and then pointed to the two computers in the back corner. "Agnes Ira."

"Perfect!" Allie said, smiling as she typed in the name.

Agnes and Ira were the two most powerful computers in the lab, and Ms. Slade was especially proud of their names. Agnes was the computer that gave love advice in an episode of an old TV show called the *Twilight Zone*, and Ira was the computer used by Wonder Woman's alias, Diana Prince. The two machines were used exclusively for special projects, and they weren't on the school network or protected by the district firewall, so no one could get past the login screen without Ms. Slade's permission.

Allie quickly typed in a bunch of fake profile data, took a picture of the whole class, and then moved on to the quiz questions. As the series of four pictures flashed on the screen behind her, Allie went around the room and gave each person a chance to answer. There were twenty-three students in the class, so she rounded the room twice and let Ms. Slade answer the last four questions.

Then Allie described the photo clues, and how Click'd worked on proximity to help you and your top ten friends find one another. She played the *bloop* sound. "This sound is unique to Click'd. Every time you hear it, it means one of the people on *your* leaderboard is within fifty feet of you. And your job is to track him or her down using the clues."

Allie looked around the room. "Any questions?"

Benita Samuels raised her hand. "I'm just curious. This looks super fun, but how is it a game for *good*?"

Allie's heart started racing again. She thought the *good* part of Click'd was so obvious. But after seeing Nathan's game . . . maybe it wasn't.

"I think the *good* will come from the stories it generates. My CodeGirls and I learned so much about one another, all because of Click'd. Sure, it's not building houses for people in need, but people need friendship, too." Benita nodded along with her.

Xander Pierce raised his hand and Allie called on him. "When can we play?"

She was about to say *Next week*, but then she thought about Benita's question. If she was going to beat Nathan, she needed to show the judges that her game wasn't only as well designed as his; she had to prove it was as inherently *good* as his. To do that, she needed real-life success stories. And lots of users. She remembered what Maddie said during lunch. Maybe she was right—there wasn't a better week to share Click'd.

If everyone in that room joined and shared it with a few of their friends, she could have fifty or sixty—maybe even one hundred—users by Saturday. That would look good to the judges. And with all those users, she'd have at least two or three interesting friendship stories to share during her stage presentation.

Before she could talk herself out of it, she looked at Xander and said, "You can start playing right now." She let her gaze travel around the room. "Anyone else want an invitation?"

Every hand in the room went up. Even Nathan's.

Allie caught Ms. Slade's expression. She could tell she was confused about her sudden change of heart, but she didn't tell her to stop or anything, so Allie kept going.

The advanced computer science class worked together on projects all last year, so she already had all their names in her contacts. She returned to her desk, opened Click'd, and began checking the boxes next to their names. She pressed INVITE.

Ms. Slade returned to the front of the room. "Okay, guys, I'm glad you're excited, but keep those phones off. We have work to do. You can start clicking after school."

Clicking. Allie smiled. She liked the sound of that. A lot. Enough to overlook all the reasons she had been waiting to share it.

She hid her phone under her desk and typed a quick group text to Maddie, Zoe, and Emma:

Allie

changed my mind

invite everyone you know

let's see what Click'd can do!

five

By the end of Advanced Computer Science, Click'd had sixteen new users. At the end of sixth, there were twenty-seven users. And more people joined throughout seventh period. Allie tried not to think about it, but it was impossible with all those strangers downloading her game and taking her quiz. Would they know how to read the clues? Would they know how to access the leaderboard?

By the time the final bell rang, there were thirty-two users. She left seventh period with a smile on her face. She couldn't wait to get home and log into the CodeGirls server so she could see what was happening on the back-end database.

Allie had barely taken ten steps when her phone let out a *bloop-bloop*.

She looked down. The screen was bright yellow, and Allie felt the adrenaline surge through her whole body. Someone was close!

She cut through the crowd bound for the bus, listening for sounds. And as soon as she turned the corner that led to the front of the school, her phone let out three *bloops* as it changed from yellow to red.

Allie stopped and looked down at the photo. She knew this girl, Claire. She sat behind her in photography class the year before, and she used to stare at her dark curly hair, envying the way it always seemed to fall in perfect ringlets. Allie could never get her curls to look like that. In the picture on her phone, Claire still had braces, but Allie remembered how excited she was when she got them taken off right before summer vacation.

Allie listened carefully. From across the grass, she heard the sound again.

She came up on her tiptoes, trying to see over the crowd, and spotted another phone high in the air. It was still at least thirty feet away, but it was moving toward her, and Allie could see the screen tinted red and flashing fast.

Her heart kicked into a whole new gear as she held her phone higher. She saw a hand waving to her, and she waved back as the two of them twisted through the crowd.

They were both smiling as they stopped in front of each other. Claire turned her phone so Allie could see the photo she'd taken with her dad on a hike a few months back. "I thought I knew you! We had photography class together last year," she said as she brought her hand to her chest. "Claire Friedman."

Allie already knew her name, and not just because they'd had a class together. Everyone knew Claire. She was an eighth grader. A super-popular eighth grader.

"Hi! Allie Navarro."

Claire gave her phone a little shake. "I just installed this thing. I have no idea how it works, do you?"

Allie beamed. "Yeah. Now we tap our phones together."

"Really?" Claire smiled even wider as she brought her phone to Allie's. Their phones vibrated and the screens flashed white, and then their leaderboards appeared. Claire's name and photo appeared in Allie's #5 spot.

"My first friend!" Claire said. Allie looked over and saw her name in the #8 spot on her leaderboard. The rest of the slots were still little blue question marks. "This is so cool! I'm going to invite all my friends." She opened her contacts and started putting little check boxes next to all the names. "I've never even heard of this app until today."

Allie took a deep breath, trying to keep her cool. "I just released it this afternoon," Allie said. Claire was bent over her phone, focused on her screen, but when Allie added, "I built it," her head snapped up.

"You what?" she asked with wide eyes.

Be cool, Allie told herself, but she was finding it hard to act like it was no big deal when it was *totally* a big deal. "I built Click'd at computer camp over the summer."

Claire was still staring like she was waiting for the punch line. "Seriously?"

"Seriously."

"Was it hard?"

Allie laughed too loudly. "Yeah. Really hard."

Woo-hoo, their phones called out. Claire looked down at her screen and laughed. "What was that?"

"That means we take a selfie. It'll go out to all the users to announce that we clicked."

"Shut up! That's awesome!" She threw her arm around

Allie and pressed her cheek to hers, and Allie tried to look relaxed, even though she was totally freaking out on the inside.

Claire took the picture and then looked at Allie again. She blinked fast and said, "Wow. Okay. Mind. Blown." Then she went back to checking boxes. "Now I'm telling *everybody* about it." She pressed the INVITE button, and then pointed to the line of buses waiting in the roundabout. "I'd better go before my bus leaves without me."

Allie followed her gaze. Her bus looked nearly full too. "Yeah, same here."

"Well, I'll see you around."

"Yeah. See you."

Allie ran to her bus and climbed the steps. As she walked down the aisle toward Zoe, she looked around. It was impossible not to notice that everyone seemed to be typing on their phones, and Allie couldn't help but wonder if they were downloading Click'd. Or maybe they already had, and they were busy taking the quiz. She couldn't believe all these kids were already playing her game.

Allie flopped down in the seat next to Zoe and pulled out her phone. "Check it out! Five down. Five to go." She turned her leaderboard in Zoe's direction.

"Ha! I'm beating you." Zoe slapped Allie's arm with the back of her hand and showed Allie her screen. "I only have the number seven slot open."

"When did you do that? School's only been out for, like, eight minutes!"

"PE." Zoe tucked one leg under the other and turned toward Allie. "You should have seen the locker room during seventh period. You would have died. None of the teachers were around, so everyone broke the no-phones rule! A bunch of girls had already installed Click'd and taken the quiz, so by the time I got there, they were already holding up their phones and walking row to row, listening for *bloops*." Allie smiled. She loved that Zoe had already adopted the sound effect like it was a real word. "A few seconds later, my phone started going nuts!"

Allie looked at Zoe's leaderboard. "I know Lizzie. She's in my science class," Allie said. "And these guys are both in my math class. Oh, and Ajay Khanna and I went to the same elementary school. Do you know him?"

"Nope, never met him before. But between sixth and seventh, I'd had my whole head stuffed in my locker, checking my stats, when my phone *blooped* and started flashing and stuff, and when I looked up, Ajay had his head in the locker right next to mine. He was watching his phone flip out, too! We started cracking up, and then we tapped phones, and *boom!* Number six." Zoe brought her chin to her chest and glanced at Allie out of the corner of her eye. "And he's kinda cute, don't you think?"

Allie nodded. "Definitely. And he's nice, too, so I think you two should be a thing, like ASAP, because I need a cute success story."

"If you insist," Zoe said with a shrug. "But only because I'm part of your street team and you need my help."

The bus pulled out of the roundabout and into the street. Allie tried not to check her phone every thirty seconds, but she couldn't help it.

"Whoa." She hadn't meant to say it. The word just slipped out.

"What?" Zoe asked.

"Sixteen people have joined in the three minutes since we got on the bus!" Allie did a little dance in her seat. "I was hoping for fifty users—maybe sixty—before Saturday's presentation, but I might have that many by *tomorrow*. Don't you think?"

"I think you'll have double that by tomorrow. This thing is moving!" Zoe drummed her hands fast on the seat in front of her, and the girl sitting there turned around and shot her a glare. Zoe apologized.

Suddenly, Allie's phone went *bloop-bloop*.

She and Zoe stared at the flashing yellow light. They listened. And they looked around, but no one on the bus seemed to be responding.

"Yellow is one hundred feet, right?" Zoe whispered.

Allie nodded.

"Then it's coming from outside."

They both heard the bus engine rumble to life. They stood, trying to get a better view out the windows. The bus inched forward, but it couldn't go very far; there were two buses in front of them, waiting to turn into the street.

Bloop-bloop-bloop.

Suddenly, they heard a pounding sound coming from

the front of the bus. "Wait!" a muffled voice yelled. The driver pulled on the lever and the doors swung open.

"Thanks!" a guy said as he climbed the stairs. He had his hand on his chest and he was trying to catch his breath. "I didn't know where to go."

"Find a seat," the driver said. And then he added, "Quickly."

The boy pulled his phone from his pocket and looked at the screen, and then he took a seat in the third row.

Bloop-bloop-bloop.

Allie watched him glance down at his phone. And then he slowly turned around.

She held her phone in the air with one hand and waved at him with the other.

He waved back. And then he twisted in his seat, and pointed at Allie as he said something to the girl behind him. She took the phone, passed it to the guy behind her, who passed it to the girl behind him. It traveled toward Allie, row over row.

Penny McCaskill was sitting across the aisle with the guy's phone in her hand. She tossed it to Allie like they were playing hot potato.

Zoe leaned in closer, her shoulder brushing against Allie's as she tapped the two phones together and watched the screens light up, side by side. Their leaderboards appeared.

Marcus Inouye. Allie looked at his profile pic. She didn't know who he was. And she was certain he hadn't taken their bus last year, because she would have remembered him.

"He's in my Spanish class. His family just moved here from Denver." Zoe tapped on his profile. "Cute pic," she whispered.

Allie felt her stomach do a little flip-flop. Yeah, it is, she thought.

"Well?" someone yelled, and Allie and Zoe looked up. Marcus was turned around, kneeling with a big smile on his face. "Where did you land?"

"Three," Allie yelled back, holding up three fingers.

He nodded approvingly. "Nice. Where am I on yours?"

"Six," Allie yelled back, and Marcus gave her a thumbs-up.

Zoe elbowed her in the side. "Dude, that was kind of adorable," she whispered.

"A little bit, right?" Allie whispered back. She was beaming as she handed his phone back to Penny, who started it up the aisle again, headed back to Marcus.

"Okay, what just happened?" Penny asked.

Zoe answered before Allie had a chance to. "Allie built it at coding camp over the summer. It matches you up with friends; *everyone's* playing it." She jiggled her phone. "What's your cell number? I'll send you an invite."

People closed in around her, calling out their phone numbers, and Allie and Zoe typed them in as quickly as they could.

Allie had pictured her best friends playing with Click'd. She'd even pictured it moving around her other circles of friends, to girls in her classes, and people she'd known since elementary school. But this was different. She'd never pictured anything like this. Not in a million years.

Zoe looked down at her phone. "They're coming in like crazy now. Look: it's up to fifty-eight."

When the bus stopped at the curb in front of Allie's house, she stood and threw her backpack over her shoulder. "See you tomorrow," she said to Zoe.

As she walked down the aisle, she couldn't help but notice that the whole bus seemed to be taking the quiz. She felt like she was on top of the world. And that must have made her feel braver than usual, too, because when she passed Marcus, she slowed her steps. "See ya, Six," she said.

He tipped his chin up and said, "See ya, Three."

six

As Allie fished her key out of her backpack, she could hear her dog scratching excitedly on the other side of the front door.

"Hold on, Bo!" Allie turned the key and heard the dead bolt click open. She barely had one foot in the door when her dog was jumping up on her, begging for his usual greeting.

"Hi! Aw . . . I missed you, too, buddy!" Allie rubbed his head as she let her backpack slip from her shoulder and drop onto the floor next to the entryway table. She sat on the tile with her legs folded in front of her, laughing as Bo jumped into her lap and started licking her cheeks. She buried her fingers in his curly brown fur. "Did you have a good day?" She took his face in her hands, looked him in the eyes and said, "Dude, I had the craziest day! I'll tell you all about it, but I swear, you're not going to believe me."

She kissed his wet nose and stood up. "I'm starving. How about you? Do you want a cookie?" She rubbed his head again. "Let's get you a cookie!"

She walked to the kitchen with Bo on her heels and took a dog biscuit from the ceramic container on the counter. He gobbled his treat and then followed Allie around the kitchen as she made a toasted cheese sandwich and poured a glass of milk.

She brought her plate over to the couch and turned on the TV. Bo snuggled into her side with his chin resting on her leg as she ate and flipped through the channels, looking for a good soccer match. She was glad none of her teachers had been mean enough to assign homework on the first day of school.

Allie pulled her phone from her pocket and launched Click'd for what seemed like the hundredth time that day, but instead of opening her Mercer Middle School group, she went back to the main screen and selected the CodeGirls group instead.

She opened the chat window and typed a message to everyone.

> Allie
> I miss you guys!

Seconds later, the messages started flooding in.

> Skylar
> I miss you too!
>
> Zaina
> How was everyone's first day?
>
> Kaiya
> Fine, but missing the fishbowl!
>
> Morgan
> 😞 the fishbowl . . .
>
> Courtney
> Did you show your friends Click'd?

Allie smiled at the screen as she typed her reply.

> Allie
> Yep. And they LOVED it. And shared it. Get this:

Allie took a screenshot of her profile and sent it to the group.

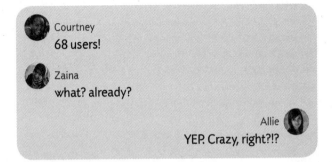

Courtney
68 users!

Zaina
what? already?

Allie
YEP. Crazy, right?!?

Allie told them all about her strategy to collect more data and real-life success stories, so she'd have even more to show the judges on Saturday.

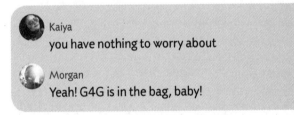

Kaiya
you have nothing to worry about

Morgan
Yeah! G4G is in the bag, baby!

Allie wasn't so sure about that. She thought about Nathan's game. She pictured all those little people marching from house to house, building something important together and making a real difference in the world. That's the kind of stuff the judges would want to see. Built was so obviously a game for good. Was Click'd?

She put her phone on the coffee table. "We need to get out of here," she said. Bo had been dozing happily, but as soon as he heard her voice, his head snapped up. "I have no idea how I'm going to make it through soccer practice tomorrow. Wanna go for a run?"

Bo knew that word well. He jumped off the couch, ran straight for the door, and sat there with his tail wagging while Allie grabbed his leash off the hook in the laundry room.

At dinner that night, Allie told her parents all about her day. "I'd only planned to share it with Zoe, Maddie, and Emma, but then in fifth period Ms. Slade asked me to present it to the whole class, and they looked so excited about it. So I shared it with all of them, too. And now look!" Allie turned her phone so her parents could see the screen. "Ninety-four users! As soon as we all get within range tomorrow, our phones are going to go crazy! Our leaderboards are going to start changing and everyone's going be running around, looking for clicks."

"Are you allowed to use phones during school?" her dad asked.

"Not technically. But we can use them before the first bell and after the last one." As soon as she said the words, her phone chirped in her pocket and she reached for it.

Zoe

Check the user stats!!!

"Speaking of rules . . ." her mom said as she pointed at Allie's phone. "Not at the table."

"Hold on. Just this one thing," Allie said as she tapped on the Click'd icon. "No. Way."

"What's wrong?" her dad asked.

Allie turned the screen and showed them her profile. "One hundred!" Allie squiggled in her chair, giggling and waving her phone above her head. "One hundred!" she repeated. "That's huge! That's like a *real* user base!"

Her mom and dad smiled at each other and her mom shook her head. "Congratulations, sweetie. Now put the phone down, please." Allie set her phone facedown on the table and reached for her fork.

Bo crawled under Allie's chair and she started petting him with her bare foot. As they ate, her mom filled them in on the company she'd been investigating all summer for the newspaper where she worked. And then her dad told them all about a new client he just took on in his law office. Allie listened, but all through dinner, she couldn't stop picturing all those people from school sitting in their bedrooms, taking the quiz she wrote. She'd watched it spread across her CodeGirls class, but that was different—those girls had practically helped her build it. The whole idea of other people—some of them total strangers—creating a profile, taking the quiz, made her feel oddly powerful. And also a little freaked-out.

But later that night, when she went up to her room and logged into the server, she realized she had nothing to be worried about. She could see everyone's profiles. She could see the Instagram shots the system pulled for clues, and the gallery of ClickPics everyone had taken so far. They all looked so happy—cheeks pressed together, arms around each other, all wearing huge smiles.

She flopped down on her bed and Bo cuddled up next to her, and then she opened her group text to Maddie, Zoe, and Emma. She felt like she was on top of the world as she typed:

Allie

Best. Street. Team. EVER!

Tuesday

seven

Click'd

Allie Navarro

142 users

The bus doors slapped open and Allie climbed the stairs.

"Hey, Three," Marcus said from his spot in the third row.

"Hi, Six," she said. She was about to ask him about his leaderboard, but when she looked up and saw what was happening on the bus, she found herself at a loss for words.

Every single person seemed to be talking, laughing, twisting around in their seat, and passing phones across aisles. Blue, yellow, and red lights flashed, and *bloops* ricocheted off the windows, one after another.

Allie walked to her seat wide-eyed. She'd expected a little excitement once all those new users got within range of one another, but this wasn't even close to what she had in mind!

"Everyone—and by that, I mean *ev-er-y-one*—is talking about your game," Zoe said. "You're famous."

A voice behind them yelled, "Anyone know who this is?" Allie turned around. A guy in the back row wearing a Warriors cap held his phone up high.

"That's Ana Hirono," someone else yelled.

A girl a few rows in front of him twisted around in her seat and waved. "Hey! I'm Ana," she said. He waved back and passed his phone to her. Everyone watched as it made its way to Ana, and then she tapped their phones together and yelled "Six and seven!" She held the phone up in front of her to take a selfie, angling it so she could see him waving his arms around in the background.

"This is . . ." Allie was at a complete loss for words. She finally settled on, "Unbelievable."

Zoe laughed. "It was like this when I got on the bus three stops back," she said as she tipped her phone in Allie's direction. "I filled that last open spot on my leaderboard as soon as I stepped on the bus, and within minutes, people who were there yesterday fell off and new ones swapped in. I gotta tell you, I think I'm a little bit addicted."

"Uh-oh. Is this going to be like your Snapchat obsession?" Allie joked.

"Maybe," she said proudly.

Zoe tapped the shoulder of a girl in front of her with thick red braids, and she turned around. "This is Lauren. She's a sixth grader. She's my number seven."

Lauren gave them an awkward wave and a shy smile. She had blue braces and wore shiny lip gloss. Then she turned around again and the girl next to her elbowed her, like having Zoe for a friend was a big deal or something.

"How is it that I have more in common with her than I do with Maddie and Emma?" Zoe whispered.

She showed Allie her leaderboard. Maddie had moved down to #8 and Emma was #10.

Allie's phone *blooped* three times and her screen started flashing red. "That was fast." The picture clue was someone's volleyball team, so it wasn't any help. Then Penny's phone *blooped* three times and started flashing red.

Penny looked down at her phone and laughed. "Do I even want to know the story here?" she asked.

Allie felt a pang of sadness when she saw the screen. It was a picture of her and Courtney with their arms around each other, gummy worms dangling from their lips.

"That's my roommate from computer camp." Allie remembered she'd spent the whole day trying to troubleshoot some issue she was having with Click'd, and she was determined to figure out the problem before she called it a night. Courtney had shown up in the Fishbowl with two Sprites from the vending machine and a huge bag of gummy worms. She sat down next to her and didn't leave until Allie did.

Penny held out her phone and Allie tapped hers against it. Then they looked at their leaderboards and watched their names settle into place.

"Eight," Penny said with a smile.

"Ten," Allie said, smiling back. As soon as the word left her mouth, her phone *blooped* again.

It was like that all the way to school, and by the time the bus pulled into the roundabout and came to a stop, Allie's leaderboard was full and there were one hundred seventy-six users.

"This is kind of crazy, isn't it?" she asked Zoe.

"Yeah," Zoe said. "Crazy fun!" She stepped into the aisle and threw her backpack over her shoulder.

"I thought it might break, you know? I was afraid it would crash with all these people hitting the system at once, but it's solid." Allie jumped off the bottom step and landed on the sidewalk, but she felt like she was walking on air. "If it keeps up like this, I could have data on the whole school by Saturday. Do you know how good that would look to the judges? Zoe, I might actually have a chance at winning this thing!"

Allie pictured herself standing on the Games for Good stage as the Spyglass CEO, Naomi Ryan, announced the winner. She imagined her parents in the front row, clapping and hugging each other, and Ms. Slade standing backstage next to the other mentors, beaming proudly. And then she pictured Nathan, standing next to her, looking shocked and defeated. She smiled to herself. She might have liked that image best.

Zoe peeled off at her classroom and Allie kept going. When she turned the corner, she saw Maddie waiting at her locker wearing a big smile and her favorite light blue V-neck tee. Maddie called it her lucky shirt and firmly believed that every time she wore it, something good happened. Allie secretly thought she liked it because it made her eyes look even bluer than usual.

"Lucky tee. What's the occasion?" Allie asked.

"Didn't you get my text?" she asked, bouncing in place.

Allie wondered how she could have missed it, but then she remembered the chaos she'd just left. "You should've seen the bus. It was madness."

"Look," she said as she showed Allie her screen. Chris Kemmerman had joined Click'd.

"You invited him?" Allie asked.

Maddie nodded fast. "Emma dared me."

"I didn't know you had his number."

"Zoe got it from her brother over the summer. They've been begging me to text him for months, but . . . I don't know, I guess I've been waiting for the right time." Allie balanced her backpack on her knee and started swapping out her books for her first three classes while Maddie kept talking. "He must have joined late last night. I checked right before I went to sleep and he wasn't in the user list, but this morning, he was!"

Maddie swayed her shoulders from side to side, and then added her hips. Allie started laughing. "What is *that*?"

"My happy dance," she said, but then she stopped suddenly. "Wait. What if he's not on my leaderboard?"

"What are the chances?" Allie asked.

Maddie navigated over to her profile and checked the latest numbers. "With two hundred twenty-five users and ten spots on the leaderboard, that gives us a four point four percent chance at clicking."

Bloop-bloop-bloop.

Maddie's phone sounded and the screen lit up bright blue. "Ooh! New friend! Gotta go!" she yelled over her shoulder as she took off running, holding her phone high above her head.

eight

Click'd

Allie Navarro

225
users

Allie took her lunch tray and made her way over to the old oak tree. She slid in between Zoe and Emma and tipped her chin toward Chris Kemmerman's table. "Well? Where is he?" she asked.

Maddie followed her gaze. "I don't know. He's taking forever."

"He'll be here. He was in math third period," Zoe said.

All their phones buzzed and Maddie said, "Ooh, a new pic!"

They all looked around for Mr. Mohr, and then Maddie checked her screen.

"Yikes," she said. She passed her phone around under the table so everyone could see the screen. Ella Samuels and Sadie Court were blurry in the shot, like they were trying not to stand too close to each other as they took the obligatory selfie. Neither one was smiling.

"That's the worst ClickPic ever!" Emma said, laughing under her breath. "Could they look more miserable?"

Zoe pressed her hands into the table and leaned in close. "They were best friends last year, but I heard they haven't said a single word to each other all summer."

"Well, I'm assuming they talked today," Maddie said. "Check it out." She lifted her phone again to show them Sadie's leaderboard. Ella was in the number one spot. "And Sadie is Ella's number two."

"See, that's because they're supposed to be friends. I know this because I'm the master quiz maker." Allie shot them all a confident smile.

"Yes, you are," Zoe said.

But then Maddie's phone *blooped* in her hands and she jumped so high, it made everyone laugh. "*Eep!* You guys. Look."

She set her phone flat on the middle of the table, screen up and solid blue. No one said a word. They were all too busy waiting for the color to turn yellow.

"Why isn't it changing?" Emma asked after a full minute.

Maddie took her eyes off the screen to scan the quad. "Because Chris stopped moving. Look, he's talking to someone over by the water fountain." She pointed to someone on the exact opposite side of the quad. He was standing next to a table full of people.

"How can you tell that's him?" Emma asked, squinting.

"It's him," Maddie said.

Allie judged the distance.

She thought back to that day she and Courtney had gone out to the Fuller University football field to try to figure out the three distances she'd use for Click'd. She tried to picture the field in her mind. If she and her friends were in the end zone, Chris might be somewhere around the forty-yard line, which would make him a little more than one hundred feet away. He was still in Click'd's blue zone, but just barely.

"You guys . . . it's him, right? It has to be him."

"It really could be anyone." Zoe barely got the words out when Chris started walking toward their table again.

Bloop-bloop.

They looked down at Maddie's phone. The screen had turned bright yellow.

"Oh my God, it *is* him!"

Chris must not have heard the first alert, but he heard the second one. He stopped, looked at his screen, smiled, and then turned slowly in place, giving the quad a solid three-sixty spin. Then he started walking again, a little more slowly, searching and listening as he went. Maddie's eyes were glued to him. The rest of the girls were watching the scene like a tennis match, swapping from Chris to Maddie and back to Chris.

When Maddie's phone let out a triple *bloop*, they all jumped and their eyes darted down to the screen. It was a picture of Chris and someone who looked like his little sister. The picture flashed faster as Chris got closer.

They all looked up when Chris stopped behind Zoe. "Hey." He turned his phone so they could see the picture on his screen.

Allie recognized it right away. The four of them were dressed in matching green shirts with matching green hats and matching green socks. "St. Patrick's Day, I'm guessing."

"Nah, just a random Thursday," Zoe said sarcastically, and Maddie shot her a look.

Chris smiled. "Well, it's a nice pic and all, but it's not very helpful." Then he looked down and saw that the phone in the center of the table had his picture prominently displayed, tinted red and flashing fast. "One of you is going to have to tell me who that phone belongs to."

"We could. But it's way more fun to keep you guessing," Maddie said, wearing that confident, flirty smile of hers.

"Here, have a seat," Zoe said as she scooted over to make room for him between her and Maddie. Chris sat. And then he reached forward and set his phone on the table, right next to Maddie's, with less than an inch of space between them.

He glanced around the table. "We had English together last year, didn't we?" he asked Emma, and she nodded. Then he looked at Zoe. "I know you. You're Quinn's little sister."

"Zoe," she said.

"Chris," he said to the whole group. "Is that your phone?" he asked, and Zoe shook her head. Then he looked at Allie. She took her phone from her pocket and showed it to him. Emma held hers up before he had time to ask. "So, process of elimination says . . . you." He glanced at Maddie.

"Maybe," she said.

He reached out, gave his phone a little nudge, and it hit Maddie's. The two phones glowed white and then flashed their leaderboards.

He stood and looked down at the phones. "Looks like you're my eight," he said.

"And you're my nine," Maddie said.

"Good. You bumped Sean from that spot," Chris said as he gestured toward his table. "That's not going to go over well."

"Why not?"

"He started off as my one this morning, but he's been slipping off the board all day. I think it's crushing his ego." He shrugged. "That's okay; he could use a little ego check anyway."

Allie stole a glance at Chris's leaderboard. It was hard not to notice that it was filled almost entirely with girls.

Woo-hoo, Chris's and Maddie's phones called out simultaneously.

"Well, I guess we should make it official." Chris reached for his phone, held it at arm's length, and leaned in close to Maddie as he snapped a selfie. Seconds later, all their phones lit up with a picture of the two of them.

He stuffed his phone in his pocket as he stood. "See you around, Maddie," he said as he walked off, heading for his table.

As soon as he was gone, Maddie's smile slipped from her lips.

Zoe noticed right away. She reached across the table and flicked Maddie's forehead with her finger. "Stop it. Right now."

"Nine?" Maddie pouted.

"How many users are there?" Zoe asked.

Maddie looked at the screen. "Two hundred sixty-three," she said.

"Right, so do the math. Out of two hundred sixty-three people, he's your number nine. What are the odds of that, Maddie?"

"Three-point-three percent," Maddie said plainly.

"Three-point-three percent," Zoe repeated. She pointed at Chris's table. "And you finally talked to him."

"Yeah."

"And he knows your name."

"True."

"And two hundred sixty-three people just saw a picture of the two of you with your faces all smashed together!"

"Now that's an excellent point." Maddie's face lit up again. She grabbed her phone and took a screenshot of the leaderboard. Then she swiped right and the photo of Chris and his little sister lit up her screen. She took a screenshot of that, too.

"He's even cuter up close," she said.

"See?" Emma said. "It's all good."

"It's all good," Maddie echoed. And then she stood and slapped her hands on the table. "Glad that's done. Let's get out of here. We have new friends to make."

The four of them walked around campus for the rest of lunch, and by the time the bell rang, Click'd had 312 users and Maddie's, Zoe's, Emma's, and Allie's leaderboards were changing every ten minutes or so.

"We're still number one," Zoe said as she turned to Allie and gave her a high five.

Emma stopped in her tracks. "What's wrong?" Allie

asked, but Emma didn't answer right away. She was still staring at her phone.

"You've all bumped way down," she said. "You two are seven and eight, and Maddie's my ten. I barely even know the rest of these people."

Maddie grabbed Emma's shirtsleeve and gave it a little shake. "That's part of the fun!"

Emma squirmed away. "They can't be my top friends over you guys! How is that even possible?"

"It's totally possible," Maddie said. "With three hundred twelve people in the system, the odds of the three of us being each other's top ten drops to three-point-one percent."

Allie looked at her out of the corner of her eye. She was good at math, but even she couldn't imagine calculating that fast in her head. "You're a freak of nature, you know that, right?"

Maddie shrugged. "It's a gift."

"Hello?" Emma waved her hands in front of them. "Doesn't anyone care about this?"

"Not really. It's not like it means anything," Zoe said.

"Of course it does." Emma crossed her arms. "How can you even say it doesn't *mean* anything?"

"It means we all answered a bunch of questions the same way, Em. That's all. It doesn't say anything about our friendship," Allie explained.

"Well, then maybe you shouldn't have named it Click'd," Emma said sharply. "Because then, you know, people might start to think it had something to do with figuring out who you click *best* with."

"Wait. Are you seriously upset about this?" Zoe asked.

Emma thought about it for a few seconds, and then she crinkled her nose and said, "A little bit. Yeah." She waved her finger around in front of the three of them. "And when we've all fallen off each other's leaderboards, you're going to feel the same way."

"I don't think I will," Zoe said.

Emma let out a huff. "You're just saying that because you and Allie are number one. But we're not even a third of the way through the school yet, so if Maddie's right, the odds of us being together will plummet every day." She brought her hand down in front of her like an airplane falling from the sky.

The three of them laughed, and that seemed to make Emma even more upset. She looked at her screen, as if her own words had just given her an idea.

"Wait . . . what if I stop playing? Then my leaderboard won't change." She looked at them. "What if we all stopped playing? If we never tapped phones with anyone else, our leaderboards wouldn't change, right, Allie?"

Allie shrugged. "You'd still get alerts when you got within range, but you could turn those off in settings, I guess."

"Okay, but why on earth would you *ever* do that?" Zoe asked as she and Maddie exchanged a look.

Emma wasn't giving up. "You guys, we don't have to do the scavenger hunt part. Let's stop playing so we can lock in our leaderboards exactly the way they are right now." She raised her eyebrows at Maddie. "That way, you and Chris won't move."

"Hey, don't bring Chris into this. The two of us are solid. We're not moving, no matter how many users join." Maddie smiled confidently.

"Besides, we can't do that," Zoe said. "The more users Allie has by Saturday, the better her chances of winning the Games for Good contest. We have to help her get players, so *they* can get new players, and *they* can get players."

"Yeah, we're Allie's street team," Maddie added, and then she turned to Allie and gave her a fist bump.

Emma thought about it for a minute and then blew out a heavy breath. "Fine. I'll keep it moving, but I'm doing this entirely for you, Allie. Because I have three best friends." She pointed to each in turn. "And I don't need to click with anyone else but you guys."

nine

Click'd

Allie Navarro

332
users

"Hey, Allie," some guy said as they passed in the hall between fourth and fifth.

"Love your app!" another girl told her when she was gathering her books from her locker.

As she was rounding the corner by the library, a guy passed her and then doubled back. "Wait! You're Allie?" he asked. And when she nodded, he waved a few people over and they all gave her high fives.

When she reached the computer lab, she opened the door and stepped inside, and everyone in the room started clapping. Allie curtsied dramatically and thanked them for sharing the app. "It wouldn't have this many users if it weren't for all of you," she told them.

She was walking toward her desk when Ms. Slade called her over. "Sounds like Click'd is a huge hit. Everyone's talking about it," she said. "How many users do you have?"

Allie pulled out her phone, launched Click'd, and opened her profile page. "Three hundred thirty-two." She felt so confident as she said it, but her expression changed when she saw the look on Ms. Slade's face. "What?" Allie asked. "Isn't that good?"

"Of course. I'm glad people are having fun with it, it's just . . ." Ms. Slade forced a smile. "It's going around *a lot* faster than I expected."

"I know, right? I was worried about stability at first, but it's working exactly the way it's supposed to." She took two steps closer. "My Games for Good demo is going to blow your mind. It'll be so much better than the one you saw at CodeGirls."

"I loved your demo at CodeGirls," Ms. Slade said plainly. "I told you then not to change a thing. Because you didn't need to."

Allie thought back to Nathan's Built demo. "Nah, it wasn't good enough. I had twenty users and a few stories from camp, but now I have more than three hundred users. And you should see what's going on out there." She pointed at the door. "Kids are using it to make friends during the first week of school and it's doing real, actual *good*!"

"It was doing good before, Allie," Ms. Slade said. But she

must have been able to tell how excited Allie was, because her expression morphed into a genuine Ms. Slade–smile. "Why don't you use your class time today to start collecting some of those stories?" she said as she pointed to the two computers in the back corner. "Nathan's using Agnes, but you can use Ira."

"Really?" Allie's eyes lit up.

It was perfect. She was dying to look at the back-end database again now that there were so many new users.

Ms. Slade reached for a pen and wrote something on a bright blue Post-it. "Here's the password. Rip that up when you're done."

"Thanks!" Allie hurried to the back of the room, flopped down into the seat, and hit the space bar on Ira's keyboard. She looked over at Nathan. He was leaning back in his chair with his head resting against the wall, his headphones over his ears, and his eyes closed.

"I can see you're hard at work," Allie said as she entered the password and pressed the RETURN key.

She wasn't sure Nathan had heard her, but then his head fell to one side and he slowly peeled his eyes open. "I'm thinking."

"Don't hurt yourself."

She wasn't as worried about Nathan as she had been when he'd showed his demo to the class. After she gathered all her new data and a few inspiring success stories, those judges would have to see that Click'd was doing just as much *good* as Built.

"Besides, there's not much to do at this point. My game is working flawlessly," he said.

"Good for you," Allie said. "So tell me, how many users do you have?"

Nathan rolled his eyes.

She cupped her hand to her ear and leaned in closer. "I didn't hear you. Did you say 'zero'? That's interesting. My game's a total hit. I have almost three hundred fifty users. And it's Tuesday. I'll probably have another three hundred by this time tomorrow. Last I heard, the judges like to see games with actual users."

"Well, they also like apps that are making a difference."

Allie let out a huff. "Click'd is making a difference!"

"Right. Of course. How did the students of Mercer Middle School go on before they knew how many other people liked pizza as much as they did?"

Nathan put his headphones back on and angled his monitor so she couldn't see it.

Allie glared at him as she turned her monitor away from him, too.

Shake it off, she told herself.

She logged into the Fuller University server and navigated over to the CodeGirls development area.

After watching the photos, profiles, and leaderboards on her phone all day, it was so cool to see row after row, column after column, filled with the data that made everything run. Allie scrolled up and down, taking everything in. She could see each user's phone number. Each person's profile photo. She had all their birthdays, favorite colors, favorite sports, favorite books, favorite movies, and favorite things to do in their spare time. She knew how many siblings each one had. She could clearly see how each person had answered every single quiz question. She even knew the password they each used to get into the system.

It made her feel a little guilty to know that much about that many people. But it made her feel a bit powerful, too.

With a few more clicks, she opened the leaderboard stats. The screen was a sea of numbers, but it didn't take her long to figure out how everyone was mapping up against one another in the system. She had access to information no one else knew. She could see each person's top ten ranking, even if they hadn't found one another yet.

That made her think about Emma's words back at lunch, so she opened her profile and studied her leaderboard. Emma seemed to think Click'd was broken—that her top ten had to be wrong—but it wasn't. It was spot-on. The numbers said so, loud and clear.

Allie started wondering about the others, so she looked at Zoe's stats, and then at Maddie's. She could tell how all three of their leaderboards would change once they got within range of some of the newest users. And she could tell that Maddie wasn't going to be happy about it.

She started sorting the data, trying to learn as much about her users as she could. She sorted them by birthday, to see who was the youngest and who was the oldest. She sorted them by number of siblings, curious to see how many of them were only children like she was. And then she sorted them by favorite dessert, just for fun.

But when she sorted all the users by grade, she noticed something interesting: of her three hundred sixty-three users, two hundred twenty-five of them were seventh graders, eighty-four were eighth graders, and only fifty-four were sixth graders.

Click'd was spreading around the school, but it wasn't reaching everyone equally. She wanted stories from all the grades. And now that she knew it was stable, she wanted all the users she could possibly get.

Maybe it needs a little nudge, she thought.

She selected all the names in the Click'd user list and typed out a message:

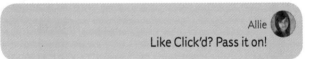

Allie
Like Click'd? Pass it on!

She added the download link and pressed SEND. There was a loud *whoosh* sound as her message disappeared from the outbox.

The bell rang and everyone started collecting his or her things and heading for the door, but Allie hung back. There was one more thing she was curious to learn about her user base.

She sorted the data again, highlighting anyone who received an invitation to join Click'd but hadn't downloaded the app.

It was a short list.

Just three names.

And one was Nathan Frederickson.

ten

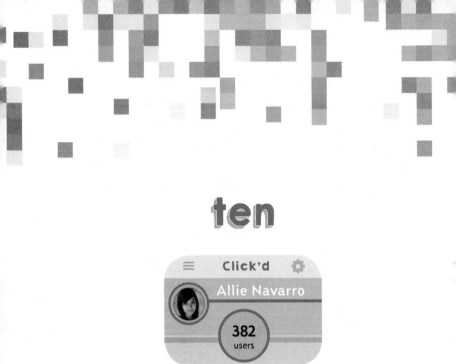

Click'd

Allie Navarro

382 users

"Whoa," Allie whispered under her breath as she stepped into the hallway and took in the scene.

As soon as the final bell rang, a bunch of people bolted from her math class and raced out the door, and everywhere she looked, she saw kids running with their phones lifted high in the air. She could see their screens changing colors and hear the *bloops* echoing off the hallways as people ran toward each other, tapped their phones together, and took a quick selfie before they took off running again, following the next clue.

She pulled out her phone and checked her own stats.

Click'd was up to 382 users, and the count was growing by the second. By the time she got to the roundabout, it was already up to 423.

All those people were playing with Click'd. With *her* app.

She was just about to step onto the bus when she heard someone shouting her name. She turned around and saw Zoe racing toward her. "Allie! Wait!"

"I have to go," Allie said, laughing. "*You* have to go, or our bus is going to leave without us." The driver watched them, looking annoyed.

"In a sec. I have to show you something first, *in private.*" Zoe grabbed her arm and pulled her away from the open windows and out of earshot.

"What's going on?"

"Have you seen Emma?"

"No. Not since lunch. Why?"

Zoe had one hand over her mouth, like she was going to be sick.

"What's wrong?" Allie repeated.

Zoe reached for her phone and handed it to Allie. "This."

"So . . . Emma told you she likes Andrew Sanders. What's the big deal?"

"This was a clue," Zoe said.

"A clue? About what?"

"No, listen. You don't get it." Zoe looked around to

be sure no one could hear, and even though they were all alone, she took two steps closer to Allie. "I just clicked with Wyatt Davies and this was the clue that showed up on his phone."

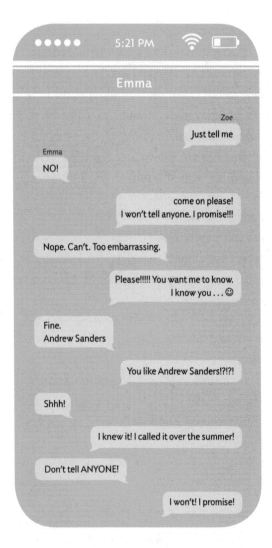

5:21 PM

Emma

Zoe
Just tell me

Emma
NO!

come on please!
I won't tell anyone. I promise!!!

Nope. Can't. Too embarrassing.

Please!!!!! You want me to know.
I know you . . . 😊

Fine.
Andrew Sanders

You like Andrew Sanders!?!?!

Shhh!

I knew it! I called it over the summer!

Don't tell ANYONE!

I won't! I promise!

Allie furrowed her brow like she was still trying to connect the dots.

"It's a screenshot. You can tell by the top, look: time, battery life." Zoe tapped her screen with her fingernail. "This conversation between Emma and me happened on Saturday night. This was from *my* phone. I *took* this screenshot."

"Why would you do that?" Allie asked.

Zoe scrunched up her nose and shook her head. "I don't know. It's just that . . . Emma never tells me anything—"

Allie cut her off. "She never tells *anyone* anything. She's *Emma!*"

"I know. I guess it just seemed like a big moment. I wanted to capture it." Zoe sighed, but then she threw her shoulders back and looked Allie right in the eyes. "Still, that's not really the point. The point is that this picture was in my photos app and *nowhere* else." Zoe glanced at the screen, grimaced, and shoved her phone in her back pocket, like she couldn't stand to look at that text for another second. "There is no way I posted that on Instagram."

"You must have done it accidentally."

Zoe looked at her sideways. "Please . . . that's almost impossible to do, Allie. Besides, if I had posted it by mistake, don't you think I would have known by now? I checked anyway, just to be sure, and it's not in my feed. I didn't send this to *anyone*. Not one single person."

Now it was Allie's turn to feel the color drain from her face. "Are you one hundred percent sure?"

"I am one *thousand* percent sure." Zoe grabbed Allie's arm. "Click'd pulled this from my photos, not my Instagram feed."

Allie pictured that specific part of the code. It had taken her almost a full week to figure out how to pull the clues from Instagram and store ClickPics in the phone's photos app, but she'd finally done it. She'd tested it hundreds of times. And nothing like this had ever happened with her CodeGirls friends. But then again, they'd spent more time testing it than they did playing it.

"It has to be a fluke. There are hundreds of users and this hasn't happened once until now." Allie's backpack fell to the ground by her feet. "But still . . ." She trailed off, unsure how to finish her sentence.

There was no way she could let this go unchecked. The text itself was bad. The fact that it had exposed Emma's secret was worse. But the real problem—if there was a real problem—was potentially much, much bigger. Sharing people's personal photos without their permission? That was in a whole new ballpark.

"What do we do?" Zoe asked.

The bus driver was motioning to them, and Allie held her finger up, asking him to wait a minute. "Only one person saw it, right? Just Wyatt?"

Zoe nodded. "And he's cool. I told him to delete it."

"Good." Allie checked the time. "You go home. I'm going to go to the lab and take a quick look at the code. If it's somehow pulling photos from both sources, I'll find it. It should be an easy fix."

"Really?"

"It's fine. No big deal." Allie sounded more confident than she felt. "I have an hour before soccer practice. That's plenty of time. I'll just ask my mom to bring my soccer bag and pick me up here instead. I'll meet you at the field."

Zoe still looked like she was going to be sick. Allie hugged her and said, "Stop worrying. I've got this. Only one person saw it, and you didn't break your promise to Emma—you didn't tell anyone—okay?"

"Okay."

"No one else will ever know."

"You don't think I should tell her?"

Allie blew out a breath. "She's already upset about the leaderboard thing. And you know how sensitive she is. I'll fix it, and then we'll tell her. Okay?"

"Okay." Zoe started toward the bus. Allie picked her backpack up off the ground and headed for the lab. But then she turned around and called Zoe's name.

"You might want to delete that screenshot," she said, and Zoe nodded.

As Allie walked to the lab, she opened her photos app and scrolled through her pictures, deleting anything she wouldn't want to accidentally share.

eleven

Allie flung the lab door open and raced inside.

Ms. Slade was sitting behind her desk. "Hey, Allie. Everything okay?"

"I . . ." Allie opened her mouth, ready to tell her everything and ask her what to do, but then she stopped herself. She pictured the look on Ms. Slade's face when she came backstage at the CodeGirls presentation. She could see the pride in her eyes that day. What would she say if she knew Allie had made such a huge mistake in the code? And then she had an even more frightening thought: What if she lost her spot in the Games for Good competition over this?

She took a deep breath and pasted a smile on her face

instead. "No . . . everything's fine. I just need to check something . . . on the CodeGirls server." She tried to look casual as she tipped her head toward the back corner of the room. "Can I use Ira or Agnes for a few minutes?"

"Sure. Ira's free."

Nathan poked his head above Agnes's monitor and gave Allie a little wave, and she scrunched up her nose. She couldn't wait until Saturday, when she and Click'd could wipe that smirk off his face.

"Are you sure everything's okay?" Ms. Slade asked.

Allie nodded. Everything was okay. It was a minor glitch. A small, easily correctable mistake. One line of code. No big deal. "It's fine."

Ms. Slade didn't seem to be buying it, but she didn't say anything else. She just smiled and lifted her hands to her ears, showing Allie her dangly earrings: two keyboard keys, a ⌘ symbol, and the letter *Z*. "Do you know what these mean?" she asked.

Allie looked from one to the other, trying to piece it together. The COMMAND key. The letter *Z*. She pictured a keyboard. "Command-Z." Allie felt her mouth turn up at the corners as she said it. "Command-Z is *undo*."

Ms. Slade nodded slowly. "See, that's one of the things I've always loved about coding. You can try anything. You can take risks. And you can fail *spectacularly*. Do you know why?" she asked, and Allie shook her head. "Because you can always hit *command-Z*. You can always *undo* it, and then redo it." She leaned in a little closer, like she was sharing a secret. "It kind of makes you wish we had a *command-Z* in life, doesn't it?"

Allie pictured Zoe's face out by the roundabout and she felt her stomach knot up all over again. "Yeah," she said. "Definitely."

"If you need any help, let me know. But remember, as your mentor, I can only look over your shoulder. I can't touch the code. I can give suggestions, but I'm not allowed to fix it for you, got it?"

Allie nodded. She was aware of the G4G rules.

Ms. Slade gave her a reassuring pat on the back. "Well, whatever it is, go *command-Z* it and make it right. And if you need my advice, you know where to find me."

"Thanks. I will," Allie said. But she didn't think she'd need it. She walked to the back corner of the room, already feeling a little better about the whole thing.

Nathan was sitting in front of his computer, with his elbows on the table, his chin propped in his hands, and a pair of bulky black headphones over his ears.

"What are you doing here? I thought your game was 'flawless.'" Allie put the last word in air quotes.

Nathan draped his headphones around the back of his neck. "It is. I'm just adding a few little touches. What are you doing here? I thought Click'd was a 'total hit.'" He put his words in air quotes, too.

"None of your business. And it is a 'total hit.' You and your little builders are toast on Saturday."

"Is that right?"

"It's a fact."

Allie took her seat and tapped on the space bar, and when the computer came to life she typed in the password and twisted the monitor away from Nathan's curious eyes.

"Hey, don't worry about me. I couldn't care less what you're panicking about." He put his headphones back on. "But I bet I know." He went back to typing as his head bobbed up and down in time with music Allie couldn't hear.

Allie glared at him. *Did* he know? How could he know *anything*? He hadn't even joined Click'd.

She ignored him as she navigated over to the Fuller University server. Within minutes, she was looking at the bright blue CodeGirls logo again. She touched it with her finger for good luck, like she could use it to channel all that knowledge from her instructor and all the words of support from her fellow CodeGirls.

She typed in passwords and opened new windows, and eventually she was in the Click'd code. She'd spent all summer staring at commands, but she hadn't looked at it since the last day of camp. Still, it felt a little bit like home. And she knew exactly where to go.

She scrolled down until she found the specific set of instructions that told Click'd to pull photo clues from each user's Instagram account. Then she found the code that told it to store CLICK-PICS in each user's photo album. Everything looked right.

Allie kept going, looking beyond those lines for anything related to photos—anything that might be causing the system to confuse the two sources—but everything looked solid. After a half hour of squinting at the screen, the lines began to blur. She rubbed her eyes, shook out her hands, and scrolled back to the top, reading every single line all over again.

"I'll be back in ten," Ms. Slade called out, and Allie and Nathan both looked up. "Need anything?" she asked, and they both shook their heads. But when she returned ten minutes later, she was carrying two bags of microwave popcorn, and she dropped them in front of Allie and Nathan. They thanked her as they reached inside.

"Everyone good here?" she asked.

"Yep," Allie said brightly, masking her concern.

"Yep," Nathan echoed as he stuffed a huge handful of popcorn into his mouth.

"Good. There's this terribly boring meeting I'm required to attend, but I'll be back in an hour," Ms. Slade said. She turned on her heel, gave them a wave, and left the lab again.

Allie reached into the bag again and went back to work, staring at the source code. The problem had to be there somewhere. Her app couldn't just pull photos from the wrong source without being told to. It would be easier if Allie knew what she was looking for.

"You know, I was thinking . . ." Nathan said as he draped his headphones around his neck.

"Nothing good can come of that," Allie said without taking her eyes off the screen. She reached for her mouse and scrolled down, wishing she had headphones of her own.

Nathan ignored her and kept talking. "I think I'm going to install this thing you made after all."

"It's not a 'thing.'" Allie still didn't look at him.

Nathan reached for his phone. "Fine, your *game*," he said, putting sarcastic emphasis on the last word. "Click'd."

Allie ignored him.

"I'm kind of curious about that leaderboard thing, you know?" When she didn't respond, he tapped his fingers on the desk, filling the silence. Then he pointed to Allie's phone. "What's yours like? Any big surprises?"

She sighed. "Install it and find out. You can see everyone's clicks." She turned to look at him and pointed at her monitor. "Look, I've got a ton of work to do here."

"Sure. Got it." Nathan poked around on his phone and mumbled to himself. Or maybe he was talking to Allie, she couldn't tell. "That invitation you sent is somewhere in here . . . Oh, wait. Yep. There it is."

Allie sighed again. Louder this time. She could hear him tapping on his screen.

"It's installing," he said.

"Awesome," she replied. Allie tried to ignore him, but she couldn't help stealing a glance out of the corner of her eye when Nathan leaned back in his chair and kicked his feet up on his desk.

"Man, you're asking for a lot of profile data here," he said as he typed. "What are you going to do with all this information?"

"Nothing."

"You could sell it. I bet a big company would pay a lot of money for this kind of stuff. We're a hot target market, you know?"

"I'm not going to sell the data."

The room got quiet again and she went back to her code. But the silence didn't last long.

"Ooh . . . photo." Nathan reached out with his arm and smiled at the camera, but when he noticed Allie had turned to look at him, he changed course. "Actually," he said as he handed her his phone, "will you do the honors?"

Allie took his phone without thinking about it, and Nathan leaned back in his chair with his hands folded behind his head, staring off into the distance.

"Seriously?" she asked. "I'm really busy here. Can't you just take a selfie?"

"Selfies never turn out."

"Sure they do. You just don't know how to take them."

"Please?" He smiled at her as he pointed to his phone in her hand. "It'll just take a second. Then I'll leave you alone."

He returned to his pose and Allie blew out a breath. She held up his phone, clicked the button, and handed it back to him without looking at the picture.

"Nice," he said, nodding approvingly. "Okay, profile done. Time for the big quiz!"

Allie rolled her eyes and then looked at the clock that hung over the door. She only had another ten minutes before her mom arrived. She told herself to focus, but she couldn't help it—her eyes kept wandering over to Nathan.

At first, his eyebrows were pinched, like he was in deep concentration, but then his face started to relax. Every so often, a smile would tug at his mouth, and when that happened, Allie involuntarily leaned toward him, dying to know what question he was answering.

Suddenly, he started laughing hard.

"What?" Allie reluctantly asked.

"Boy bands? Seriously?" He was still trying to catch his breath as he twisted the phone toward her.

"Yeah. Why?"

"Wow. Okay. Hmm. Well, this one is definitely a tough question." He drummed his hands on the table. "Pick a *favorite*. Come on, that's just crazy talk. How am I supposed to pick a single favorite boy band singer?"

Allie rolled her eyes. She wondered if Ms. Slade had any headphones she could borrow.

"You know, I'm going with Zayn."

"You do that."

"I don't really know why, I guess he seems like the most interesting one. And you know, I like that he left One Direction to go out on his own." Nathan kept talking, but Allie ignored him. "Or maybe it's just because his name is so much cooler than mine. Zayyyyn . . ." he said, drawing it out. "That's fun to say. Zayyyyn . . . How come I got a boring name like Nathan and he got a name like Zayyyyn? Maybe I should go by Naaaate?"

Allie grabbed the sides of her monitor with both hands and pretended to smack her forehead against the screen.

"Nah. You're right. I can tell by the look on your face. That doesn't have the same ring to it, does it?"

Allie sat up and pointed at her screen again. "I am trying to concentrate, *Nate*." She didn't draw it out the way he had.

"Sure. Right. Sorry."

Allie looked back at her monitor and tried not to look over at him again, but he was making that pretty impossible.

"Last question!" Nathan said in a singsong voice. "No! You're making me pick a favorite doughnut? Sprinkles, maple bar, glazed, or chocolate iced. Allie!" He slapped the back of his hand to his forehead as he looked up at her. "This test is impossible. You know that, right?"

"Are you mocking me?"

"Not at all. Look at me. I'm stumped. Totally and completely stumped." His finger hovered dramatically over his screen, as if he had a serious choice to make and feared picking the wrong one.

"You're mocking me."

He smiled at her. "I'm messing with you, not mocking you. There's a difference. Here we go." He made a big show of pressing the LET'S GO! button.

And as soon as he did, Allie's phone said *bloop-bloop-bloop* and the screen lit up, flashing fast with a red-tinted photo of Nathan and someone she assumed must be his mom. Nathan's phone echoed with the same sound.

"Well, isn't this interesting!" Nathan said as his face

broke into a huge grin. Allie craned her neck, trying to see his screen, but Nathan twisted away and curled his body over it, hiding it from her view.

She hoped it was something from Instagram.

She couldn't handle the idea of it being anything else.

Because then she'd have to tell him why she was sitting next to him in the lab.

Nathan rotated the phone in her direction.

"Nice pic," he said.

"Thanks." Allie smiled, remembering the night she posed for it. "Courtney, my best friend at CodeGirls camp, took it when we were working late one night in the Fishbowl."

She sighed. She missed the Fishbowl. She missed the people in it even more.

His eyebrows pinched together. "The Fishbowl?"

"Yeah. That's the name of the computer lab at Fuller University. It's surrounded by these super-tall windows on three sides, so while you're working, you kind of feel like you're outside. There's a small field where we all played soccer during breaks. And we'd sit in the shade under this big willow tree and eat our lunch."

Nathan smiled. "Sounds nice."

"Yeah." Allie let out a long sigh. "It was." She turned and looked at him. "It was quiet, too. People respected each other's work time."

Nathan looked at her. And then he smiled. "I feel like

you're trying to tell me something, but . . ." He lifted his phone into the air. "Okay, so what do we do now?"

"We tap our phones together to see where we landed on each other's leaderboards."

Allie reached out toward him, but Nathan pulled back. "What if we don't tap them together?" he asked. "What if we keep it a secret?"

She lowered her arm. "Fine with me. I don't need to know." She dropped her phone on the opposite side of her desk, as far away from Nathan as possible, and went back to work. Nathan set his phone down, too. And then he pulled his headphones over his ears and his fingers started flying across the keys.

Allie checked to be sure he wasn't watching her, and then she looked back at her data. All she had to do was search for his name and she'd be able to see every single answer to every single question. In a matter of seconds, she could figure out exactly where he ranked. She scrolled up to the search field. She was just about to type in *N* when he said, "Okay, I take it back. I can't stand it." He reached for his phone.

Allie wrapped her arms across her chest. "No. You didn't want to find out, so we shouldn't find out."

"Come on . . . look." Nathan fake-pouted and turned his phone so she could see his leaderboard. "I don't have a single friend."

"There's a good reason for that."

"Please?"

Allie hated the idea of giving in to him, but she also wanted him to use Click'd. She wanted him to know what he was up against on Saturday. It was an intimidation tactic, plain and simple.

"Fine," she said as she picked up her phone and tapped it against the side of his.

And then they both stopped talking or moving or breathing, and watched their screens. They flashed white. And then their leaderboards appeared.

"Did you answer the questions honestly?"

"Of course I did. Why would I lie?"

More than five hundred people in the system, and she had the *most* in common with Nathan Frederickson? That seemed impossible. Totally and completely impossible.

"Interesting score for two people who hate each other," Nathan said.

Allie glared at him. "You don't hate *me*. I hate *you*! I've hated you since . . ." She trailed off, remembering all the little things over the years, each adding up to her calling Nathan Fredrickson her archenemy. Her nemesis.

Nathan looked at Allie.

And Allie looked at Nathan.

Now she had a new reason to get more users. The more there were, the faster he'd be bumped off her leaderboard.

"I have to get back to work," Allie said.

twelve

Click'd

Allie Navarro

574 users

Allie's mom picked her up in front of the school. As she climbed into the car and slipped her seat belt over her shoulder, Bo poked his head in between the seats and started licking her face.

"Bo!" She buried her face in his neck and inhaled his soft fur. "I missed you! How was your day? Did you miss me, too?"

Allie was glad Bo was there. It helped her ignore the sound of her phone buzzing in her back pocket with new member alerts.

"Why did you have to stay late?" her mom asked as she

put the car in gear and pulled away from the curb. "It's only the second day of school."

If Allie had found and solved the problem in her code, she might have told her mom everything, but under the circumstances, she couldn't stand the idea of bringing it up. "Just working in the computer lab, getting ready for Saturday." Which was kind of true, but not completely.

She was expecting her mom to press her for details, but instead she reached over and grabbed Allie's hand. "You were so brilliant last weekend. I can't wait to see you up on that stage, in front of all those people." She shot her a smile. "We are so proud of you." And then she returned both hands to the steering wheel and started talking about some drama at work. While Allie listened to her mom's story—offering the occasional *What?* and *No way!* at the appropriate points—she stole a glance at her phone.

Click'd was spitting out picture after picture, slideshow-style, of all the people who had clicked at school that day. They all looked happy. They were all having fun. None of them seemed worried about the clues they'd received on their phones. She wanted the thing with Zoe to be a fluke or a random error, but she knew that was impossible. And after hours in the lab, she didn't have a clue how to fix it.

What was she going to say to Zoe? What were they going to say to Emma?

Her mom pulled up next to the fence that lined the field. "Maddie's mom is giving you a ride home," she said.

Allie grabbed her soccer bag from the backseat, kissed Bo good-bye, and then stepped out of the car. "See you at home," she told her mom as she closed the door.

Most of her teammates were already huddled up in the corner of the field. She spotted Maddie and Emma standing with a big group, chatting as they stretched, but Zoe was sitting alone, a few feet away from everyone else, still lacing up her cleats.

Allie dropped her bag on the ground and collapsed next to her, flat on her back. It was still warm and sunny, and she stared up at the sky, looking for animal-shaped clouds.

"You're not exactly reassuring me here, Al."

Allie closed her eyes and rocked her head from side to side. She could feel those tiny artificial pellets from the turf digging into her scalp, but she didn't care. When she opened her eyes, Zoe was staring down at her. "Turns out, it's harder than I expected."

"Speed it up, ladies!" Coach yelled as she pointed at the rest of the team, already starting laps around the field.

Zoe blew out a breath, untied her cleat and started over, buying time so they could keep talking. She motioned with her hand and shot Allie this *keep-going* look.

Allie sat up, unzipped her bag, and pulled out her own cleats, filling Zoe in as she started lacing them up.

"I can't find it," Allie whispered.

"What do you mean you can't find it?"

"I only had an hour. I'll try again tonight. But . . ." Allie looked around to be sure no one else could hear her. "All the photo-related stuff is in this one area, smack in the middle. It might not be a simple tweak to a single line of code, like I thought. Everything's interconnected." Allie interlaced her fingers. "The photo access is part of a much longer string of commands—the way it feeds users the Instagram clues, stores the ClickPics, and sends them to the whole community—it's all tied together."

Zoe still looked confused.

"It's like a three-layer cake," Allie explained, stacking her hands one over the other. "And the photo-related stuff is the middle layer. I can't just take it out without destroying the entire thing."

Allie stood and brought her foot to her hip, stretching out her leg. Zoe stood next to her and stepped her right foot forward into a lunge.

"Even if I find the issue, I'm not sure I can risk it. Not until after the competition on Saturday."

"But that's four days away." Zoe stepped back and lunged on the other side.

"Exactly. It's *only* four days away. I went through the system and deleted anything that looked suspicious—all the screenshots, all the blurry photos, basically anything that looked like it wouldn't have been posted—but I only found a few. It's not consistently using the photos app as a source for the clues. Ninety-nine percent of the time, it's pulling them from Instagram, exactly the way it's supposed to."

"Okay, but what about the other one percent?" Zoe looked around to be sure no one could hear her. "If you ask me, you got lucky. What if there's something, like, really personal?"

"Then I'll delete it from the queue before it goes out."

Zoe let out a laugh. "What are you going to do, spend the next four days glued to a chair, watching a computer screen, just in case Click'd pulls a random pic?"

"I'm going to be glued to a chair until I can figure out how to fix it, anyway. I'll be going straight to the lab at every lunch and right after school, and when I get home, I'll go straight to my desk and comb through the code. I might as well look for sketchy photos while I'm at it. What other choice do I have?"

"You could take it down," Zoe said. "Not forever or anything . . . just until you find the issue and fix it."

Allie had already thought about that, but she couldn't bring herself to do it. Not when Click'd had so much momentum. "I've got this. It's going to take longer than I thought, but I can fix the code, and in the meantime, I'll make sure it doesn't share anything from anyone's private photos again."

"Ladies!" Coach yelled as she pointed to the rest of the team, already on their next lap. "Are you planning to join us today?" The two of them took off running, keeping their distance from the others.

They ran in silence for the next few minutes.

"So do we tell Emma?" Zoe finally asked.

Allie made a face. "She'll be so upset."

"Right?"

"Besides, it sounds like Wyatt was cool about the whole thing."

"Totally. He deleted it."

"So Emma's secret is safe. What's the point of upsetting her, you know?"

Zoe shook out her hands. "I can't even imagine telling her."

"Then maybe we don't."

thirteen

Click'd

Allie Navarro

605
users

When Allie got home from soccer, Bo was waiting in the entryway just like he always was. Allie dropped her bag on the floor and sat down so he could jump into her lap and cover her face with kisses. "Come on," she said to him. "Let's get to work."

He followed her as she raced for the staircase and started up, taking them two at a time.

"Where are you going?" her mom called from below. "What about dinner?"

Allie stopped and gripped the banister. "Can I eat up in my room?"

Her mom looked over at the kitchen table. Allie's dad

was already there, setting three plates on top of three place mats, and filling three glasses with milk. "Have a quick dinner with us. We want to hear about your day."

No, you don't, Allie thought.

She'd already been away from Click'd for two hours, and even though no one was likely to be close enough to trigger a photo clue that late in the day, she couldn't stand not working on the fix.

"I have a *ton* of homework."

Her mom thought about it, and then she finally pointed at the kitchen table, and said, "Fine. Grab your plate to go."

Allie went into the kitchen and took a big whiff. Everything smelled delicious, and she suddenly realized she'd barely eaten lunch and hadn't had anything but microwave popcorn since. She kissed her dad on the cheek, and then scooped out a huge helping of chicken, rice, and steamed vegetables.

"Bye," she called back as she ran for the stairs. The scents teased her all the way into her room.

Allie sat in her chair and Bo crawled underneath her desk and curled himself into a ball at her feet. Since she left the lab, 47 people had joined, leaving the count at 605. She shook her head in disbelief. At the rate she was going, she'd have 650 users by morning and maybe even 700 by the end of the next day!

She took bites of food while she scanned over all the data she'd gathered over the last thirty hours. And then she tapped on the photos tab and scanned the queue. A few people had clicked while she'd been at soccer practice, and she smiled when she looked over all the new ClickPics, wondering how they'd found each other. Did they hear *bloops* while they were at the mall? Did their phones call out to each other during football or track practice?

She went through each of the photo clues, one by one, but they looked like they'd been pulled from Instagram. It all seemed innocent enough.

"Maybe it magically fixed itself," she told Bo as she buried her toes into his soft fur. And then she let out a heavy sigh, because she knew that was impossible.

Allie navigated back to the Fuller University site, but she couldn't quite bring herself to click on the CodeGirls logo. She was dreading the plunge back into the sea of commands; she'd already swam through the source code four times that day. She turned around and looked at her bed, wishing she could crawl inside the sheets. Instead, she reached for her phone, launched Click'd, and opened her CodeGirls group.

Her profile page looked the same, except she had 20 friends instead of 688. She wished she'd created a teleportation device instead. If they could all just beam themselves into Allie's bedroom, they'd have this problem solved in no time.

She opened Courtney's profile and read through her stats, even though there were no surprises there.

Over the summer, the two of them started playing this game they'd made up called "good day/bad day." At times, CodeGirls Camp could be an emotional roller coaster mixed with triumphant highs and intense lows. So, before they fell asleep at night, they'd each list the top three things that had gone right that day and the top three things that had gone wrong.

Allie opened the chat window and typed a message.

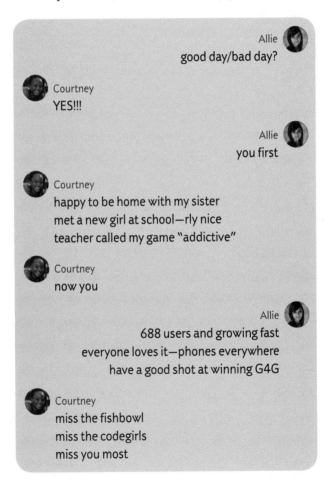

Allie
good day/bad day?

Courtney
YES!!!

Allie
you first

Courtney
happy to be home with my sister
met a new girl at school—rly nice
teacher called my game "addictive"

Courtney
now you

Allie
688 users and growing fast
everyone loves it—phones everywhere
have a good shot at winning G4G

Courtney
miss the fishbowl
miss the codegirls
miss you most

Allie wanted to tell her about the glitch in Click'd, but after that, she wasn't sure how to do it. Instead she kept it simple.

Allie returned to the Fuller University server, clicked on the CodeGirls logo, and navigated over to Click'd's source code. She blinked a few times as the colorful text filled her screen, and then she brought her fingers to the keyboard. "Okay, bad code," she said. "I'm tired. And I'm done messing around. I'm not going to stop until I fix you. Got it?"

Wednesday

fourteen

Allie sat down next to Zoe on the bus, let out a long exhale, and dropped her head on Zoe's shoulder. Zoe patted it and asked, "No luck?"

"I was up until midnight. I fixed the issue in the code, but every time I tested it, it caused a problem somewhere else. It's going to take a little longer."

"Well, I deleted all my pictures, just in case."

"Yeah," Allie said. "So did I."

Allie closed her eyes and the two of them rode the rest of the way in silence. Every once in a while she'd hear a *bloop-bloop-bloop* and see a phone make its way around, but most of the people on Bus #14 seemed to have found each other. Between the gentle rocking and hum of the engine, Allie almost drifted off. But when the bus pulled into the roundabout and she and Zoe stepped off, she suddenly felt wide-awake again.

The bus might have been quiet, but the campus definitely wasn't; the scene on the front lawn was even crazier than it had been the day before. Everyone was running around, dashing past the roundabout and disappearing into the hallways. They were tapping phones, snapping selfies, and comparing leaderboards. And Mr. Mohr was standing in front of the office with his arms crossed, watching the whole thing. Until the bell rang, there was nothing he could do about it.

Allie walked to her locker feeling pumped with adrenaline. But when she turned the corner, she saw Maddie waiting there, staring at her phone and looking upset.

"Chris is gone," Maddie said as soon as Allie was within earshot.

"What?"

Maddie spun her phone around. "Look. Gone. Emma, too, and you and Zoe are down to nine and ten. I barely know the rest of these people!"

"That's part of the fun, remember?" Allie said as she gave Maddie's shirtsleeve a shake, just like Maddie had done to Emma the day before. But Maddie's face fell, and Allie could tell she wasn't in the mood to joke about this. "Hey, don't worry. You're probably still his number six."

"I'm not. I checked. I'm gone from his leaderboard, too."

Allie went back to swapping out her books.

Maddie rolled her eyes and leaned back against one of the lockers. "You don't get it, Allie. You weren't here last summer. Zoe and Emma know . . . I've been waiting for months for a reason to talk to him and I finally did, and now it's just . . . so . . . over!"

"No it's not," Allie said, nudging her with her shoulder. "Look, Click'd got you two talking. That's the hard part, right? Who cares if your status has changed? Just go up to him and say something like, 'I miss your face . . . on my leaderboard.'"

Maddie started cracking up. "Seriously? 'I miss your face'?"

"No," Allie said, laughing along. "You've gotta get that pause in there, and then really deliver the rest of it." She tried it again. "You have to say, 'I miss your face—pause—on my leaderboard.' It's not the same without the pause and the second part."

Maddie started laughing even harder. "Not that I have a clue about *any* of this!" Allie said, still giggling. "You're the flirt, not me. Gotta run." She shut her locker and gave Maddie a wave. She started to walk away when she heard Maddie say, "Allie! Wait."

When Allie stopped and turned, Maddie stepped in closer.

"As much as I appreciate the flirting advice," she said, still giggling, "and trust me, I do, I kinda had another idea."

"Yeah?"

"I was thinking . . . You know, I'm *real-life* best friends with the developer of Click'd."

Allie looked at her sideways. "True. And?"

"And, so, I get perks."

"Perks?"

"Yeah, I thought, maybe . . . you could go in and, you know, tweak a few things?"

"Tweak a few things?" Allie repeated. She looked at Maddie like she must have misunderstood her.

Maddie clasped her hands together, pleading with her eyes, and Allie laughed again, even though she knew that wasn't the reaction Maddie was expecting.

"No way."

"Come on! *Puhhhhllllllleeeeeeese!*" Maddie begged, stepping in closer, but Allie kept shaking her head. "It wouldn't hurt anything and no one has to know. Just change a few of my answers to match his? Just change my ocean to forest and my noodles to pizza, and like, change ten more things so we have more in common than anyone else."

"No." Allie couldn't believe what she was asking.

Maddie combed her fingers through her hair. "Okay, fine. Can you at least tell me what number he is now? Because seriously, how am I supposed to sleep at night without knowing? I mean, what if he's my eleven? Then you may only have to change, like, two or three things. That's it. That's *nothing.*"

Allie hung her head, but she could tell Maddie wasn't ready to give up.

"I can't do that."

"But what if he's my *eleven?*" she repeated, gripping Allie's arms with both hands. "Which reminds me, why can't we see past the top ten?"

"Because I thought it would be more interesting."

"Interesting? That's not *interesting!* That's evil."

Allie snarled as she wiggled her fingers in front of her and let out an evil laugh, trying to make Maddie smile.

"Stop it!" Maddie swatted at Allie's fingers, but that only made her wiggle them harder.

Then Maddie folded her arms across her chest. "Fine. Okay, I have another idea! Don't change anything. Just look at Chris's quiz answers and tell me what he picked.

I'll delete my profile, go back in, and answer the same way. That way you're not changing anything!"

Allie pictured the database, filled with columns and rows of information. Hundreds of names and cell phone numbers, answers to more than fifty personal questions. "First of all, he would totally notice if you fell off his leaderboard and then suddenly reappeared. Think about it," Allie said as she tapped her finger against her temple. "And second of all, that's cheating."

Maddie laughed and threw her hands in the air. "Cheating? Who cares? It's not like you created a game to reverse the effects of climate change. It's a friendship app. And you said it yourself, it's all for fun."

"It is."

"Well, it was a lot more fun when Chris Kemmerman's name was on my leaderboard."

fifteen

Allie only planned to be in the quad for five minutes, six tops, just long enough to grab her lunch, swing by the table to say hi to her friends, and tell them she had to get to the computer lab to get ready for the Games for Good competition on Saturday. It was only half-true, but only Zoe would know that.

As Allie waited in line for her lunch, she couldn't help overhearing the chatter around her. People seemed to have come up with a whole new language to talk about Click'd:

Elizabeth was my three and I was her five, but now she's my five and I'm her eight.

Aidan and I were ones yesterday, and now he's not even on my leaderboard!

Eva and I have been twos from day one! Haven't budged! Allie turned around as two girls high-fived each other.

Bloop.

Allie heard the sound coming from her back pocket. She grabbed her tray from the lunch window and headed out for the old oak tree, and as she walked she could feel her phone buzzing; she couldn't wait to get to the table so she could check the screen.

Bloop-bloop.

She looked around. The coast was clear, so she stopped right in the middle of the quad, pulled out her phone, and right as she did, the screen flashed red and the *bloop-bloop-bloop* sounded. She looked up, expecting to find her match, but instead, she found herself nose to chest with someone much taller than her. She slowly tipped her chin up.

Mr. Mohr held a small orange bucket in his outstretched hand. Something inside was *blooping* three times.

Allie stuffed her phone in her back pocket as fast as she could, but it triple-*blooped* again. The phone in his bucket called out to hers in response.

"Sorry. I—" she began, but Mr. Mohr cut her off.

"No, don't be sorry. You're making this a really good day for me." He looked at his watch. "The bell only rang ten minutes ago and I'm already up to seven phones." He held his hand out flat. "I'll take it, please."

"No . . . really . . . I promise it won't happen again."

He tapped a fingertip against his open palm and looked down at her with his eyebrows raised. Allie scanned the quad and saw a bunch of people watching the two of them. Mr. Mohr might have let her off with a warning, but with an audience and a point to prove, there was no way he'd do that.

"You can pick it up at the end of the day."

Allie reluctantly dropped her phone into his hand. When he tossed it into the bucket, her phone must have touched the one that had been *blooping*, because one of the phones let out a shrill *woo-hoo!*

Mr. Mohr peered inside. "What was that?" he asked.

Allie shrugged and shot him a *how-am-I-supposed-to-know* look.

Mr. Mohr looked like he was about to say more, but then his gaze settled on something over her shoulder. "Hmm. Another one," he said as he gave the bucket a little shake, like he was determined to fill it to the top before lunch ended.

He walked away and Allie squeezed her eyelids tight. But then she opened them and shook it off. It didn't matter, she reminded herself. She could live without her phone. She had everything she needed in the computer lab.

When she arrived at the table under the oak tree, Allie slid in between Zoe and Emma. "Mohr just took my phone," she said with a huff.

She was expecting a little sympathy, but no one said a word. Then she looked at Zoe and realized she was staring back at her with wide eyes, as she shook her head and mouthed the word *bad*.

Allie didn't get it. She looked across the table at Maddie, who was sitting there with her arms crossed, glaring at her.

"Hold up. You're not actually mad at me for refusing to rig your leaderboard?" Allie asked, and Maddie slowly shook her head and pointed at Emma.

Emma was staring down at the table. She wasn't speaking. She wasn't even moving.

"What's wrong?" Allie asked, even though she had a sinking feeling she already knew.

"Wyatt didn't delete it," Zoe said. "He sent it to tons of people."

"No," Allie whispered.

Emma's head snapped up. Her eyes were red and puffy. "No?" she yelled. "Seriously? That's all you can say? *No?*" She pulled out her phone and shoved it under Allie's nose.

And there it was: the text exchange Zoe showed her on the lawn the day before. The same one Allie had deleted. The same one that was responsible for the stomachache Allie felt that whole day before, and the one that seemed to have resurfaced again.

Zoe jumped in. "Allie tried to help. It wasn't her fault, it was mine. I'm so sorry. I never should have taken the screenshot of our conversation. I guess I was just so glad you told me, you know—that you trusted me with a secret. You've never done that before, and I guess . . . I just . . ." Zoe trailed off when she realized she was rambling and making it worse.

Allie jumped in to try to rescue her. "Don't be mad at Zoe. It's not her fault. It's mine. That picture never should have gone anywhere! As soon as she told me what happened, I deleted it from the system, and after that, I spent hours in the lab after school, trying to figure out what happened."

Emma kept her eyes locked on Allie. She didn't blink. "I'm not upset about the picture—"

"Oh, good!" Zoe cut her off with a sigh. "Because I know it's embarrassing, but—"

Emma slapped her hand hard on the table. "I *am* upset about the picture! I'm mortified and humiliated. But that's not what I'm *most* upset about." She pointed at Allie and then at Zoe. "You both knew yesterday. You saw me at soccer practice, after this all happened, and you acted like nothing was wrong. You both knew and neither one of you told me."

"We didn't think anyone else would see it." Zoe looked at Allie for support, and Allie tried to nod, but inside, she was cringing.

"In other words, you didn't think I'd find out?" Emma asked accusingly.

Zoe squeezed her eyes shut and then opened them and locked her gaze on Emma. "I didn't *want* you to find out, because I felt horrible and I didn't want to hurt you. Wyatt

133

said he was deleting it, and I honestly thought that was the end. I didn't think he'd send it to anyone."

Emma took a deep breath and folded her arms across her chest. "Well, he did. As it turns out, he thought it was pretty hilarious, so he sent it to all his friends. And they sent it to all *their* friends, including Andrew. And now the entire school knows something I told exactly *one* person." She held her finger up in front of Zoe. "One person I trusted."

"I'm really so—" Zoe began, but Emma held her finger up in front of her face.

"I know. I get it. You're sorry." Emma shook her head. "Do you know where I was when I found out?"

Allie and Zoe looked at each other, and Zoe whispered, "No."

"I was in the girls' locker room," Emma said. "I was standing there in my underwear, when Megan Braxton shoves her phone in front of me and says, 'Aww . . . so cute!' And everyone laughed. The entire row. Because they'd all seen it already, and it was pretty clear I was the only one who hadn't. So I know you're sorry, Zoe, and that you never meant for this to happen, Allie, but it did. And it happened to me. So no, I'm not going to accept your apology right this second."

Allie felt like someone had just punched her hard in the chest.

Emma had been holding back her tears, but they started slipping down her cheeks quickly and she wiped them away as fast as she could. She stood and reached for her backpack. "You know what would have made it a teeny, tiny bit better?" she asked. "If anyone—say, for example, one or *two* of my best friends—had warned me first. *That* would have been better. Then I would have been prepared with some snappy comeback or ready to totally deny it, but to be surprised like that . . ." Her voice caught and she sucked in a breath. "I wasn't even wearing pants!"

Emma stormed off, wiping her face as she left. Allie tried to swallow the lump in her throat, but it wouldn't budge.

None of them knew what to say, so they sat there for almost a full minute until Maddie broke the silence. "How could you guys do that to her?"

"It was an accident," Allie said.

"We didn't think she'd find out," Zoe whispered.

"Please stop saying that. Do you have any idea how messed up that sounds?" Maddie asked.

"She was already upset about the leaderboard thing, remember? We didn't want to make it worse," Zoe added.

Maddie pressed her hands flat against the table and stood. "Just FYI, if I tell either one of you a secret and you tell anyone else, accidentally or otherwise, even if you don't think I'll ever find out, and even if you think you fixed it, I want to be the first to know."

Maddie dumped her untouched lunch into the closest trash can and ran off after Emma.

sixteen

Click'd

Allie Navarro

765
users

"I'd better go talk to her," Zoe said as she stood from the table. "You coming?"

Allie pictured the lab and the empty seat in front of her computer station. "I know I should, but I need to get back to work. People are already clicking." She hooked her thumb toward two girls on the far end of the quad, sneaking their phones from behind their backs and tapping them together on the down-low.

Zoe waved her off. "Go. This is my fault anyway, not yours." Allie started to jump in to disagree with her, but before she could say anything, Zoe turned on her heel and took off in the direction Emma and Maddie had gone.

Allie left the table, and as she walked by each group of friends, someone looked up and waved at her, or called out, "Hi, Allie." She waved back. All these people suddenly knew who she was. If she weren't feeling so horrible about what happened with Emma, she might have been a little more excited about it.

She opened the door to the computer lab and immediately saw Nathan in the back corner. Again. She groaned under her breath. She was hoping to have the lab to herself.

Allie crossed the room, collapsed into her chair, and pulled the keyboard toward her. She was typing in her password when Nathan leaned closer, right into her personal space.

"Allie Navarro, you're the most famous person at Mercer Middle School," he said, pretending to hold a microphone to his mouth. "What do you think about all this attention?"

Allie couldn't look at him. It was all she could do to keep from screaming. Just twenty-four hours earlier, she'd sat in this seat and told Nathan her app was a hit. She bragged about how many users she had, and she couldn't believe how perfectly everything was going. Everywhere she looked, people were playing her game or talking about it. Now, two of her best friends were furious with her, and Allie knew they were right to be. She should have told Emma.

"You don't have any words for your adoring fans?" he asked, pushing his imaginary microphone under her mouth again as he cocked his head to one side.

She pushed his hand away.

"Hey . . . you okay?" he asked. He sounded genuinely concerned.

Allie shook her head. She wasn't okay, but she didn't feel like talking about what happened, and she certainly didn't feel like talking about it with Nathan. Besides, she didn't have time to chat; she had too much work to do.

"I . . . messed something up with one of my friends, that's all." Allie could hear her voice trembling. She sucked in a breath and changed the subject. "What are you doing in here, anyway?"

"Big lunch date," Nathan said, and then he tapped his hand against the side of his monitor. "Agnes and I kind of have a thing going."

"That's not at all weird." The back of her neck felt tight, so she took her fingers off the keys and brought them to her shoulders instead, pressing them deep into her skin. "What about Cory and Mark?"

Nathan shrugged. "I don't really hang out with them anymore."

"Really?"

"Yeah. Why is that so surprising?"

"It's just that back in elementary school you guys were like brothers." Allie shot him a half smile. "Remember that one year, on the first day of school, when all three of you were in tears because you were in different classes?"

Nathan cleared his throat. "First off, that was third grade. And second, Cory and Mark were in the same class and *I* was in a different one." He rested his hand on his chest. "I was the only one crying. But hey, thanks for bringing it up." He shot her a half smile and added, "Good times."

She smiled back at him before she went back to her screen. He returned to his, too, but she noticed he didn't put his headphones back on.

"So what happened with you guys?" Allie asked as she deleted a blurry photo of someone's dog.

Nathan kept his eyes on his screen, too. "I don't really know. Cory and Mark started playing basketball during lunch and made a bunch of new friends, and . . . I guess I wasn't good at that."

"At playing basketball?"

"No, at making new friends."

Allie felt her chest tighten, but she didn't take her eyes off her monitor. She kept scanning the photo queue, but there wasn't much to see. Word must have gotten around about Mr. Mohr's orange bucket.

"Nothing happened, really; it just got awkward, that's all. And I was working on my game during lunch anyway, so it didn't really matter."

Allie stopped what she was doing and looked at him. "Wait a second." She pointed at the little animated characters walking around on his screen. "Are you saying you spent every lunch last year in this room, with Ms. Slade, working on your game?"

He laughed. "Well, when you say it that way you make me sound like a loser."

"I didn't mean . . ." Allie stammered. "I don't think . . ."

"Whatever. I don't care. I like my game. These little animated people make sense. Real people don't always do that, you know?"

Allie put her elbows on the armrests and leaned closer to him. "I get it. I swear, I do. And that's the whole point of my game, you know? It's supposed to make it easier to make new friends." She pointed at his phone. "I bet your new best friend is on your leaderboard right now. How many people have you clicked with since you installed it yesterday?"

He crossed his ankle over his leg and pulled on a frayed part of his jeans. Then he looked up at her from under his eyelashes and smiled. "Still just the one."

Allie looked at him. "Really?"

He angled his phone so she could see the leaderboard. Her name was at the top, and the other nine slots were still filled with question marks, exactly the way they were the day before.

"Why?" she asked.

He shrugged and set his phone facedown on the desk. He opened his mouth to say something, but then, suddenly, the door flew open.

"There you are!" Maddie yelled. She stepped inside, but Allie couldn't tell from the look on her face if she was still angry at her.

"What are you doing here?" Allie asked.

Maddie waved her phone in the air. "I thought you

should see this. There are a bunch of new users." She clicked on one of the profiles in her friend list and turned the phone toward Allie. "Do you know who this is?"

Allie looked at the picture. She couldn't place her. "I've seen her before."

Maddie laughed under her breath. "Yeah, you definitely have."

She handed Allie her phone so she could get a better look. "No way," Allie said.

"Yep. That's Ariana Grande," Maddie said. "There are a bunch of others, too. Apparently, if you play your cards right, you can have Justin Bieber, Beyoncé, Miley Cyrus, and Lady Gaga on your leaderboard, too."

Allie didn't care so much about the fake accounts. She was mostly watching Maddie, trying to get a read on her. Was she still mad about what happened with Emma? Allie couldn't tell for sure. But then Maddie smiled and said, "Anyway, I thought you'd want to know right away, so I . . . tracked you down."

It was her way of breaking the tension. Maddie hated conflict; she could never stay mad at anyone for very long.

"Thanks." Allie looked over at Nathan. He already had his headphones back on and he seemed to be concentrating on his screen, so she turned back to Maddie. "Hey, is Emma okay?" she whispered.

"Yeah. She's embarrassed. And she's mad. But you know Emma, she won't stay mad at you forever."

Allie bit down on her lower lip. "And you?"

Maddie shrugged. "I said what I had to say. We're good."

Allie shot her a grateful smile and then looked over Maddie's shoulder at her screen again. "When did you find these fake profiles?"

"About five minutes ago. Zoe and Emma were talking, and I didn't want to get in the way, so I went into the bathroom and thought I'd check for new users, and that's when I saw them. I'm guessing there's at least twenty."

Allie buried her face in her hands. She didn't have time for any of this. She was supposed to be building her user base and collecting stories that proved Click'd was a game for *good*, not fixing broken code, deleting suspicious pictures, and dealing with fake accounts.

She glanced up at the clock over the door. The bell was going to ring any second.

"I'm going to have to get rid of them one by one," Allie said matter-of-factly.

Allie's fingers flew across the keyboard. She could feel Maddie watching over her shoulder as the names, photos, numerical rankings, and phone numbers filled the screen.

"Man, you've got dirt on the whole school," Maddie said.

Allie clicked the top of the column and sorted all the users by last name. She started scanning, stopping to delete a famous person every time she saw one. She'd only deleted two of the accounts when the bell rang.

"Ms. Slade won't let you stay," Nathan said. "Trust me, I've tried."

The fifth-period students were already filing in through the doors and heading to their computer stations.

"Look, they aren't hurting anything," Nathan said as he pointed to the screen. "Don't worry about it."

"I can't just leave it like this," Allie said. "The judges are going to see this on Saturday. What will they think?"

Nathan shrugged. "That your user base is made up of a bunch of middle schoolers," he said matter-of-factly.

Allie opened her mouth to object, but she couldn't think of a comeback.

"Seriously," Nathan said. "It's not a big deal. Let it go."

Allie stared at Taylor Swift's profile data, thinking that Nathan was probably right. She had bigger problems to solve. Still, she highlighted Taylor's name, photo, and the rest of her data, and hit the DELETE key.

Then she looked over at Maddie. "You're his twelve. He's your fifteen."

A slow smile spread across Maddie's face. "Really?"

Allie nodded.

Maddie looked at her sideways. "That's not why I came in here today. You know that, right?"

Allie wasn't sure she was telling the truth, but it didn't matter that much. She just didn't want her to be mad at her anymore. Emma's anger was punishment enough.

Maddie wrapped her arms around Allie's shoulders from behind. "Thank you," she said as she squeezed her hard.

Allie stole a glance at Nathan. He looked confused as he logged out and reached for his backpack.

seventeen

Click'd

Allie Navarro

784
users

A crowd had already formed at the office counter.

"I'm going to miss my bus," one guy said.

"My mom is waiting for me at carpool," a girl behind her said. "She's probably texting me right now."

"This is stupid," a guy on her left whispered under his breath.

On the one hand, Allie was glad she didn't have soccer practice after school so she could stay in the lab as late as Ms. Slade would let her. But on the other hand, she wished she had soccer practice so she could talk to Emma. As she stood in line waiting to get her phone back, she started wondering if she could do both. If she could get Emma to meet at the lab, she could show her the Click'd database and all the code, and explain how she was fixing the issue. She could apologize for not telling her about the glitch right away, as she should have.

She couldn't wait to get her phone back.

Finally, Mr. Mohr walked out of his office carrying the orange bucket and looking triumphant. He stepped up to the counter and started sliding the phones down to the waiting students one by one. "I can't keep you from using these before the first bell or after the last one, but you know the rules. If I see a phone during the school day, it's all mine."

Allie's must have been at the bottom, and when she finally spotted it, she didn't even make eye contact with Mr. Mohr; she grabbed it and raced out of the office.

As soon as she turned it on, a text popped up on the screen. It was sent to the whole Click'd community:

LEADERBOARD PARTY!
BLACKTOP!
NOW!

"Leaderboard party?" she said under her breath. She guessed it meant a bunch of people would be in one spot, generating picture clues at the same time, and that meant she needed to get to Ira. Fast.

But first, she had to see if Emma would meet her.

> Can you meet me in the computer lab right now?

There was no reply for a full minute. Allie started walking to the lab, watching her screen as she went. Finally, her phone chirped.

Emma

Can't. Guitar lesson.

She could tell she was still angry from the tone of her text. As she walked, she typed a message to Zoe.

> Emma's still mad at me.
> Did you talk to her?

Zoe

Yeah. Still upset but she accepted my apology

She'll get over it.

But still, you should talk to her

I'm trying. She doesn't want to talk to me

Did you fix the glitch yet?

Allie knew she should have told her about the four blurry pictures, the two unflattering ones, and the two text exchanges she'd deleted during lunch, but she didn't.

Almost. Working on it now.

Allie pulled the lab door open.

Well, I don't think Emma will accept your apology until you do

"Great," she mumbled to herself. Then she pocketed her phone and stepped inside.

Allie expected to see Ms. Slade behind her desk, but she wasn't there. Nathan was hiding behind Agnes's monitor as usual, with his headphones over his ears and his forehead practically pressed into the glass. He didn't even look up as she slid into her chair and typed in Ira's password.

She went straight to the photo queue, figuring she'd focus her energies there until the leaderboard party was over, and then she'd go back to fixing and testing the code again.

But as soon as Allie landed on the photo queue, she could practically see her plans sprout wings and fly out the window. There were two screenshots in the queue—both of fairly boring text exchanges—along with a picture of Eric Valente standing in his bedroom in a pair of green-and-blue plaid boxers.

"Oh my God," she said, and immediately wished she hadn't. She turned to Nathan. She could hear the music through his headphones, and she was glad he had the volume up.

She deleted both screenshots and then clicked on Eric's picture, but with all those people in one place, the queue was moving a lot faster than it usually did—adding new photos and sharing new clues every ten seconds or so—and by the time she selected his photo and pressed DELETE, she wound up deleting the next one in the queue by accident. Her heart was racing as she toggled over to the catalog of photos that had already been sent out as clues, and saw Eric's picture right on top.

"No . . ." Allie muttered.

There was only one thing she could do.

She quickly navigated back to the database, found Eric's name, and clicked on it, drilling down into the underlying data. There, she could see his leaderboard stats and tell that he hadn't located match #7, but that the two of them were actively looking for each other.

With a few more clicks, she could tell that "someone" was Abigail Brenton.

She did another scan of the queue. It was adding new ClickPics and sharing clues even faster now. She figured there must have been at least sixty people playing out on the blacktop.

Allie went back to the main screen, highlighted Eric's and Abigail's names along with all the information stored in the database, and hit DELETE.

She pictured the two of them running around, searching for each other when suddenly, their screens went black. They'd go back to their home screens to relaunch Click'd, and they'd be prompted to join all over again, to start fresh.

Allie knew she had to go out there and find them, to tell Eric what happened and make sure Abigail hadn't taken a screenshot and sent the ClickPic to anyone.

But she couldn't leave. Not with the images coming in and leaving as quickly as they were. She turned her head to the right. Nathan's music was still blaring and his eyes were glued to his screen.

Allie looked at the photo queue again. And then back at Nathan. She had no other choice.

When she tapped Nathan's shoulder, he lowered his headphones and draped them around his neck.

"Can I ask you a huge favor?"

He pointed at his screen. "I'm kind of in the middle of something," he said, but he must have been able to tell from the look on Allie's face that this was a big deal, because his expression softened and he lowered the volume on his music. "Are you still worried about those fake accounts?"

Allie hid her face in her hands. "I wish. That's nothing compared to this."

As quickly as she could, she explained what had been going on with the photos, and how she'd been monitoring the queue to be sure nothing else got through. She was expecting him to look surprised or maybe even smug, but instead he said, "So that's why you've barely left this room in two days."

Allie nodded.

"Would you just watch this screen for the next fifteen minutes? Delete any picture that looks like it might not have been posted on Instagram. If it's blurry, if anyone's making a weird face or looks otherwise bad, or if it looks personal, delete it. If you see a screenshot of a text or any saved snaps, delete those, too."

"Got it," he said, and as soon as Allie stood up, Nathan scooted over into her seat and put one hand on the mouse and the other on the DELETE key.

Allie opened the door and the warm breeze hit her smack in the face. She ran through the quad and over to the cement staircase that led to the large blacktop area next to the field, and when she saw what was happening below, she stopped cold.

She was wrong about the count. There were a lot more than sixty kids gathered on the blacktop. Some were racing back and forth, taking selfies, and tapping their phones together. Others were clustered together in smaller groups, looking at one another's phones.

And they were still coming. As soon as a new person arrived, Allie could hear *bloops* bouncing around in the air. Her phone was in her back pocket and she could hear it calling to the others, trying to echolocate, but she ignored it—as hard as it was. She didn't have time to play. She had more important things to do.

When she reached the bottom of the steps, Bryan Nieto spotted her. "Allie's here!" he shouted. She and Bryan had known each other since kindergarten, and they used to be good friends in elementary school, but they hadn't talked much since they got to Mercer. He looked like he was about to say something to her, but then a girl stepped in front of him and threw her arm around Allie. "Hi, I'm Jess. This leaderboard party was my idea! What do you think?"

Allie clenched her jaw and forced a smile. "Awesome."

"We've all decided we should do this every day until the whole school has clicked! I'm so glad you came. Zoe didn't think you'd make it."

She tipped her head toward a group over by the grass, and Allie followed her gaze. Zoe was sitting on top of a table, talking with Ajay. Allie couldn't help but wonder if she'd been in that same spot when they were texting each other only fifteen minutes earlier.

"Can we take a selfie?" Jess asked, snapping Allie back to reality. Before she could answer, Jess was holding her phone high in the air and resting her chin on Allie's shoulder. "Thanks!" she said as she skipped off.

Soon, Allie was surrounded by people. She didn't know most of them—they looked familiar from classes and stuff—but that didn't seem to matter.

They started telling her stories, without any prompting. Blake and Jackson told her they used to be best friends in kindergarten, but they drifted apart until Click'd brought them back together. Kira and Sean said they hadn't met until they landed at the top of each other's leaderboards, but they've been inseparable all week. Ben and Brody were both new kids and neither one knew a single person on Monday, but now they had each other and a whole new friend group.

Allie listened to all their stories. She asked if she could take their pictures to use in her presentation, and they immediately started posing for her.

All the attention made her giddy. She felt like a rock star. Or a superhero. Or a superhero rock star.

Then she pictured Nathan back in the lab doing the real superhero work, protecting the innocent by scanning and deleting, and she knew she had to get back to him. But she had to find Eric and Abigail first.

She spotted Abigail standing with her friends, and Eric under the basketball hoop, staring at his phone. Allie waved them over and explained everything. Eric thought it was hilarious. Abigail did, too. And Allie wasn't certain, but it looked as if they both went straight to their photos and started deleting any they wouldn't want to share.

As she walked away, she could hear music playing and everyone chatting, and she wished she could join them.

She was at the top of the stairs, heading into the quad, when she saw Kaila Boyd, Holly Cline, and Claudia Jasper standing in a small circle next to the cafeteria.

"This is a picture of the two of you at the beach last weekend!" Kaila yelled as she held her phone up to them. Allie couldn't make out the photo, but she could tell the phone screen was flashing red.

None of them had noticed Allie yet, so she ducked behind the closest wall and listened.

"We're sorry," Claudia said.

"We really are," Holly added.

"It's one thing to go somewhere without me, but to make up a whole story?" Allie peeked around the corner as Kaila pointed at Holly and said, "You told me your mom got sick, so the trip was canceled." Allie could see Holly's shoulders sink. "So what? You just lied to me?"

"I'm sorry," Holly said. "I didn't want to hurt your feelings."

Kaila held her phone up in the air again. "How would this *not* hurt my feelings?"

"We weren't trying to be mean, I swear," Claudia said.

"We just wanted to go to the boardwalk," she added, as if that explained everything.

"Yeah," Holly said. "And none of the rides fit three people. We would have had to take turns all day."

Kaila let out a laugh. "That's okay. I get it. Better to just lie to me about it," she said sarcastically, and then she turned on her heel and stormed off.

Allie couldn't see the picture in question, but she was pretty sure if she had watched it go through the queue, it never would have occurred to her to delete it.

eighteen

Nathan slid over and gave Allie her chair back.

"See anything sketchy?" she asked.

He made a face. "People take some weird pictures," he said, "but no, everything looked legit."

Allie wondered how many pictures were slipping out there without her even knowing it.

She had to fix it. But she didn't know how. And she couldn't ignore that anymore.

Nathan didn't say anything, but he didn't have to. He knew Click'd was broken. He could tell the judges. He could win G4G.

"Are you close?" he finally asked. She knew what he meant.

"I don't know. I found the problem last night. I spent hours tweaking the code and testing it, but I can't get it to pass. Every time I think I've fixed the photo issue, something breaks somewhere else. It's all interconnected," she said, interlacing her fingers together. "I can recode all the photo-related stuff, but not by Saturday."

The room got quiet while Allie waited for Nathan to give her a lecture about the Games for Good rules. He was going to have far too much fun with this, and she was dreading every second. But then, he looked her right in the eye and said, "The store isn't charging for paint."

"What?" she asked.

Nathan tilted his monitor in her direction. She could see his little characters running around the neighborhood, carrying ladders from one house to another, dashing back and forth across the street, and speeding into the hardware store.

"It was working fine. But then I made a bunch of little changes last week—minor things, just cleaning up code and stuff." He clicked the mouse a few times and zoomed in on the store. She could see the rows of supplies—bins filled with tiny bolts and screws, shelves displaying hammers and screwdrivers, and big push brooms lined up against one of the walls—and once again, she found herself in awe of the details in his imaginary world.

She watched as a woman with blond hair and a red

sweatshirt stepped up to the counter holding a bag of nails, and the man behind the counter totaled her purchase. Her player information appeared in the corner of the screen, and as soon as he clicked on the register, fifty points were deducted from her total.

"It's charging for nails and screws and tools, but as soon as someone comes in and buys paint, it doesn't charge them. And paint is the most expensive item."

"Who's going to notice that?" Allie asked.

"The judges. All they have to do is look at my error logs."

"You have error logs?" she asked.

"You don't?" Nathan asked. Allie shook her head.

If she'd had error logs, she would have known about the photo glitch before Zoe had. She would have had a trail to follow. Instead, she had no clues at all.

A little animated character in a blue cap stepped inside the hardware store, grabbed a hammer from the wall of tools, and took it to the register.

"So that's what you were trying to fix yesterday?"

Nathan nodded. "Yeah. And the day before. And pretty much all last weekend."

Allie shot him a sympathetic smile. "What does Ms. Slade think?"

He shrugged. "I haven't told her. I was kind of hoping I could figure it out myself."

"Yeah," Allie whispered. "Same here."

Allie looked back at her screen, staring at the lines and lines of code stretched across her monitor. She knew she needed to get back to work, but the thought of poring through all those commands again made her head hurt. She was certain there was a solution, or even a simple work-around, but she was starting to think she'd never find it.

Then she looked back at Nathan's screen. It reminded her of a game she'd built last year, where players ran a dog-walking service and had to figure out how much they needed to charge to keep the dogs safe and still be profit-able. The graphics weren't anywhere near as sophisticated as Nathan's, but the game logic was probably similar.

She felt herself leaning in closer. She watched a guy in a little green hat step up to the counter, holding a bucket of paint, and then walk away with the tiny can swinging by his side and his point total unchanged.

When she looked at Nathan, she realized his eyes were locked on her monitor.

"I have a crazy idea," she said.

"I bet it's not as crazy as mine."

They looked at each other.

"I made this dog-walking game last year."

"I've solved a bunch of interdependent code issues in Built over the summer."

"I mean . . ." Allie shrugged. "I'm sure you could solve it on your own, but—"

Nathan cut her off. "Exactly. You'd fix it eventually, but—"

"Sure. But I'm just so tired of looking at it," Allie said.

"Same," Nathan said. "Ms. Slade's always telling us to check each other's code, right? So we have a 'fresh pair of eyes' on the problem."

"Exactly."

They didn't say anything after that. They just stood up and switched seats.

"How do I know you're not going to sabotage my game?" Nathan asked.

Allie shot him a smug grin. "Because there's only one thing I want out of Saturday's competition: to beat you fair and square."

She unplugged his headphones and handed them to him, and then she reached into her backpack and grabbed her own. She was glad she'd remembered to bring them.

nineteen

Allie and Nathan worked until after seven o'clock, when Ms. Slade finally said, "Okay, that's enough excitement for one day. Shut 'em down."

The two of them logged out and followed Ms. Slade to the front of the school. Allie spotted her mom's car right away. There was another car parked behind hers, and Allie assumed that must be Nathan's ride.

"Talk later?" he asked.

"I'll be back online as soon as I eat dinner. I have a bunch of homework to do, but once I finish it, I'll get back to looking at your stuff."

He held his fist out and she gave it a bump.

Allie sat down and buckled in as Bo poked his head up from the backseat and started licking her cheek. "Hi, boy!" She kissed the top of his head and stroked his ears. "I missed you so much! As soon as this competition is over, we'll get back to real life, okay? I promise. Three-mile runs. Snuggles in front of the TV. And treats. Lots and lots of treats."

Bo licked her face again like he agreed with her plan.

"How was your day?" her mom asked.

She pictured Emma at the lunch table—puffy-faced and red-eyed—and it felt like someone had punched her hard in the chest. "Fine," Allie lied. And then she asked, "How was yours?" changing the subject as quickly as she could.

She continued the strategy all through dinner, keeping the focus on her parents so she wouldn't have to talk about her fight with her friends, the fake accounts, or the glitch she still hadn't fixed. And as soon as dinner was over, she rinsed off all the plates, loaded the dishwasher, and sprinted back to her bedroom.

She worked on her math homework, read a chapter on the American Revolution for her social studies class, and did an online science quiz. As she worked, she checked the photo queue, but everything was quiet. Every once in a while, she'd picture that look on Emma's face again and she'd feel sick to her stomach.

Two hours later, she was ready to get back to the Built

code. She pulled out her spiral-bound notebook and flipped to Nathan's login instructions.

Once she could see his code, she scrolled down to the lines specific to the way the store worked, and started analyzing the commands.

Everything looked right. The lines specific to paint were identical to all the other supplies.

Bo was curled up under her feet, and he didn't budge for the next two hours as she tweaked the code and ran it through her debugging program. She moved to the next layer and the next layer, peeling the code back like an onion, testing each one.

Her eyelids felt heavy, but she couldn't stop. Not yet.

She needed a distraction, so she picked up her phone, opened the chat window, and typed a message to Courtney.

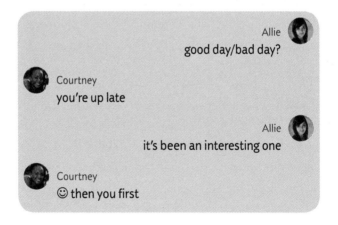

Allie
good day/bad day?

Courtney
you're up late

Allie
it's been an interesting one

Courtney
☺ then you first

Allie thought about everything that had happened that day. She wasn't quite sure how she was going to narrow it down to three good things and three bad ones.

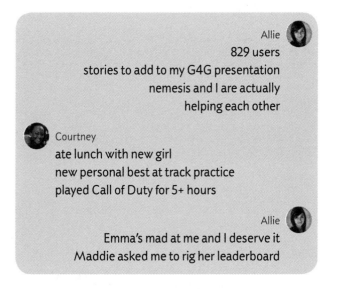

Allie
829 users
stories to add to my G4G presentation
nemesis and I are actually
helping each other

Courtney
ate lunch with new girl
new personal best at track practice
played Call of Duty for 5+ hours

Allie
Emma's mad at me and I deserve it
Maddie asked me to rig her leaderboard

Allie thought about her third item. She wanted to tell her everything that was happening with Click'd, but she wasn't sure where to start. And it was late. So she kept it simple:

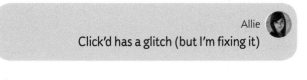

Allie
Click'd has a glitch (but I'm fixing it)

A few seconds later, her phone chirped.

Courtney
miss playing soccer on the lawn
miss our dorm room
still miss you most

Allie
♥

Courtney
♥
Goodnight

Allie
Goodnight

Allie looked back at her monitor. Those never-ending lines of code and database tables were blurring before her eyes.

She looked down at Bo. "Do you want a treat?" she asked, and Bo stood up and wagged his tail. "Come on. I need hot chocolate."

The house was silent as she tiptoed down the stairs and into the kitchen. While she waited for her water to boil, Allie gave Bo three dog snacks, and then reached into the jar and stuck another handful in her sweatshirt pocket. When her hot chocolate was done, she grabbed her mug off the counter, and climbed the stairs with Bo right on her heels.

She returned to her desk, and Bo curled up next to her feet again. While she sipped her hot chocolate, she studied Nathan's code, starting from the top again.

She spent the next hour reviewing everything, line by

line. She made a few more changes and ran more tests, and when they failed again, she decided to call it a night.

Allie was just about to log out, when she had another idea.

She had been focused on the store-specific commands, but now she scrolled way down to the bottom, into the interactions between characters. And that's where she spotted something unusual. The store was charging for paint. That wasn't the problem. The problem came much later in the code.

It was almost 1:00 a.m. when she texted Nathan.

Allie

> you told the system
> to credit all characters
> for paint

Nathan

what?

> the code is right. it's
> charging them. but later,
> it's giving them a refund

that's impossible

> check it out

Allie copied the specific line of code, pasted it into the text, and pressed SEND.

There was no response from him right away, but a few minutes later, her phone buzzed.

Nathan

Allie

working?

I think so

hold on

okay refresh

Allie hit ⌘-R and then relaunched his game. She selected a player in a red sweatshirt, clicked on the store, and watched her cross the street and step inside. She double-clicked to see the activity.

The little red character walked to the register, paint can swinging by her side, and set it on the counter. A second later, it deducted five hundred points from the account. She grabbed the paint off the counter and walked out of the store.

Allie was smiling when her phone rang. She answered it as fast as she could, and hoped her parents hadn't heard it; they'd be furious if they knew she was still awake.

"I remember what I did." Nathan launched in without even saying hello. "When I was first working on the character interactions, I didn't want to deal with transactions, so I wrote code to bypass the store fees. I thought I'd deleted them over the summer, but I guess I missed one. I bet it hasn't been charging for months and I just hadn't noticed it."

"Makes sense," Allie said.

"How did you find that?"

"I'm good," Allie said smugly.

Nathan laughed into the phone. "Yes, you are."

"Any luck with mine?" she asked.

Nathan took a deep breath. "Sort of. I'm still working on it. You're right—it's super complicated and everything's interconnected—but I think I have an idea."

Allie yawned loudly into the phone. "What?"

"Let me play with it a little longer. I'll tell you tomorrow."

"Okay," Allie said. "I need to go to bed before I fall out of this chair."

Allie could hear him typing on the keyboard in the background. Then the sound stopped. "Allie?" Nathan said.

"Yeah."

There was silence on the other end. "I'm . . . It's just . . . well . . . Thanks."

Allie smiled to herself. "Glad I could help. Return the favor, would you? You're kinda my only hope, here."

"Yikes. No pressure," he said. Allie could tell he was smiling on the other end of the phone.

"Good night," she said.

"'Night," he said.

She set her phone on her desk, changed into her pajamas, and went into the bathroom to wash her face and brush her teeth. When she returned, there was a message waiting on her phone.

Nathan

Does anyone ever
call you Allie-gator?

She rolled her eyes at the screen.

Allie

No

Hmm. OK

Why?

No reason

She didn't know what to say, so she typed:

You're weird

I know

She was smiling as she climbed into bed. Bo jumped up on top of her comforter and settled in next to her, and she rested her hand on his back as she let her head sink deep into her pillow. Her eyelids felt heavy, and her whole body was ready for sleep, but her mind was still wide-awake. She'd been so busy all day, she hadn't given Emma much thought, but now, lying there in the dark, quiet room, she couldn't get her voice out of her head.

She reached for her phone.

I miss you, Em

I should have told you

I'm so sorry I didn't

She wasn't expecting a reply, but the message bubble popped up on her screen and she could tell Emma was writing back. She must have been having trouble sleeping, too.

Emma

meet me in the library
at lunch?

Allie let out a sigh of relief as she replied.

I'll be there

Thursday

twenty

Click'd

Allie Navarro

836 users

It's going to be a good day, Allie thought as she stood waiting for the bus.

Nathan had an idea to help her fix the glitch. She had three success stories to build into her presentation: Blake and Jackson, Kira and Sean, and Ben and Brody. And by the end of lunch, Emma would have forgiven her and they would be back to normal.

But between first period and the lunch bell, things went from bad to worse.

In science, Bianca Singh told her that there was a

mistake with the leaderboard, because Alyssa Moran seemed to be stuck in her #2 spot and the two of them despised each other.

She ran into Lea Cho between second and third, and she pulled Allie aside and told her she needed to do something about this sixth grader who thought they were real-life best friends and kept sending her annoying texts.

In math, she overheard Jesse Grant bragging about all the fake accounts he'd opened.

In the passing period after third, she stepped into the bathroom and overheard two girls fighting about a picture on Click'd. One of them was screaming and the other was crying, so Allie hid in a stall until they left.

And in PE, Jane Templeton said she was working in the office and a bunch of teachers had come in to complain to Mr. Mohr about a new game that was going around campus. "They said it was disrupting their classes. None of them mentioned your name or Click'd," Jane said, "but someone's going to rat you out eventually."

Allie knew she had to face facts: She couldn't keep up. People were getting to school early, sneaking out their phones during class, and meeting up after school to click. It was becoming impossible to manage the photo queue. She'd had it under control on Tuesday, but now, with this many users, the odds had shifted.

She changed into her gym clothes and then stuck her head in her locker to type out a message to Nathan.

I'm running out of time.

Need that idea. FAST!

When the lunch bell rang, Allie walked straight to the library. Emma hadn't told her where to go, but she didn't have to. She knew her favorite spot.

She walked past the checkout desk and the banks of computer terminals, up the stairs, and over to the sunny corner window in the back by the travel section. She spotted Emma right away, curled up in one of the colorful beanbag chairs with her head resting against the glass and her face buried in the pages of a thick book.

"Hey," Allie whispered.

"Hey," Emma said without looking up.

"What are you reading?"

Emma angled the book so Allie could see the cover.

"Haven't you read that already?"

"Twice." Emma pulled her knees to her chest, and then played with the pages, gently curling them toward her, and then letting them drop. She still hadn't made eye contact with Allie.

"What are you doing in here? Why couldn't we just meet at our table?" Allie asked.

Emma slowly shook her head. "People keep making kiss noises at me. In the halls. In class. It'll die down, I'm sure, but until it does . . ." She trailed off.

"Jerks," Allie said under her breath.

"And nobody's at our table anyway. Zoe has spent every lunch playing your game—I swear, she's completely obsessed with it. And Maddie is having lunch with Chris today."

"Chris Kemmerman?" Allie asked.

Emma found a loose thread on her sweater and twisted it around her finger. "Yeah, we were group texting last night and Zoe dared her to ask him if he wanted to meet up at lunch. She did, and he said yes."

"You guys texted last night? Without me?"

"We knew you were working on the fix. We didn't want to bug you."

Allie's heart sank deep in her chest. Click'd was supposed to bring her friends together, not tear them apart.

"It's still not fixed, is it?" Emma asked, changing the subject.

Allie pulled up a giant red beanbag chair and settled in next to Emma, resting her cheek against the opposite window. The sun was shining brightly outside, and the glass felt warm on her skin. "I'm working on it, but . . . no. Not yet."

Emma shifted in her seat. "I deleted all the photos from my phone last night," she said. "And so did Maddie. I'm just curious. . . . When did you and Zoe delete yours?"

Allie thought back to their conversation on the bus the

day before. "On Tuesday night after soccer practice," she admitted.

"Because you know you can't fix it." Emma said it more like a statement than a question, and Allie shrunk into the beanbag chair, feeling small. "What if something *really* personal gets out there? I mean, my secret crush on Andrew is one thing, but what if a picture gets shared that's seriously embarrassing, or hurts someone's feelings, or like, ruins someone's life?"

"It pulls from personal photos maybe one percent of the time. I'm watching and deleting them from the queue before they go out. I haven't caught all of them, but I've caught most."

Emma dropped her book on her lap and looked Allie in the eye. "Why don't you just shut it down? You have more than eight hundred users. That's plenty of data for Saturday. Shut it down, focus on collecting stories, and fix the code next week."

Deep down, she knew Emma was right. But she couldn't imagine doing that. She'd made something important. She wasn't ready to let it go. People loved Click'd; they'd told her so. They told her on the bus. They'd stopped her in the halls all week. They'd leaned over the aisles in every class to fill her in on their leaderboard status, or to tell her about an unexpected connection. Sure, a few people had started complaining, but most of their issues would be gone along with the glitch. She knew she could fix it; she just needed a little more time.

"I can't. . . ." Allie said.

"Can't or won't?"

Allie sucked in a deep breath. "Won't. Not yet."

"Fine." Emma pulled her phone from the back pocket of her jeans and held it flat in front of her. She tapped on the Click'd icon, with its light blue background and stick-figure friends. Allie thought she was opening it, but instead, she held her finger down and didn't let go.

All the icons wobbled and a little "X" showed up in the upper left-hand corner.

Emma clicked on it and a pop-up message appeared on the screen. "Deleting this app will also delete its data." Emma said, reading the screen aloud. "Delete or cancel?"

"Please don't," Allie whispered.

Emma brought her fingertip back to the screen and selected DELETE.

And just like that, Click'd was gone.

Emma looked right into Allie's eyes. "You're one of my best friends. You'll always be one of my best friends. And I accept your apology—I really do—but if you can't fix the glitch, I think you should shut your game down." She stuffed her phone back in her pocket and returned her attention to her book. "I don't want to talk to you until you do."

twenty-one

Allie went straight to the lab and slid into her seat next to Nathan.

"There you are. I was just about to text you," he said. "I have good news."

Allie let out a relieved breath. "Please. I *so* need good news right now."

He tapped on the keyboard a few times and pulled up her code. "I looked at the edge cases—the contingency plans that tell your app what to do if the code doesn't execute the way it's supposed to—and look." He pointed at the screen. "When the program calls Instagram and can't find it for some reason—which happens all the time, right, because the server is busy, or a user doesn't have an account, or whatever—it's pulling from their personal photo stream instead."

Allie stared at the monitor. He was right.

"It seems like an easy fix, but I agree with what you said before about not having enough time to unravel everything since it's all interconnected. Changing it now might cause something else to break. So, here's my idea. Don't fix it."

"Excuse me?"

"Don't fix it until after G4G. For now, here's the faster way to solve the problem." He scrolled down to the bottom of the screen. "Get rid of the ClickPics."

"What?" Allie shifted in her seat. "I can't do that. Everyone loves the ClickPics!"

"I know, but look . . ." Nathan pointed at the monitor again. "If you just delete these lines and rewrite this one, you're no longer touching the photos app at *all*. You'd be pulling exclusively from Instagram. It's not storing or sending anything out from the photos app, so there's no risk of confusion."

He scrolled back up to the top and Allie looked over the lines again. She hated the idea of losing the Pics, but he had a good point. "I'd have to change all the app's behavior after two people click."

"No more *woo-hoo*," Nathan said with a smile, but Allie didn't smile back.

She kept going, pointing at the monitor and talking through the steps out loud. "If I remove this line, users will see the flash and the leaderboard, but the camera won't launch. Then I can just revoke access to the photos app completely."

"Exactly. Then you're just dealing with Instagram and the pictures you know people have made public. You can always bring ClickPics back once you've fixed it the right way, you know? Roll it out in a week or two. Call it an upgrade."

Allie sighed as she thought about all the work in front of her. She hated the idea of simplifying her app. She loved Click'd exactly the way it was. She didn't want to lose the Pics or the *woo-hoo*—that was her favorite part! And all the stories she'd planned to share during the competition were based on those photos.

But she had to admit it: Nathan was right. Deleting the ClickPics would be a much simpler fix. She thought back to Emma's words in the library. She didn't want anyone else to get hurt. And she needed her friend back. She had to do *something*.

"I ran a bunch of tests last night. It worked every time. Here." He slid her a printout with the specific lines of code highlighted in blue. "These are the lines you need to delete. That one in green needs a little tweaking to tie everything back together." He'd written down the specific changes to the code in neat block printing.

Allie looked over at the clock. Lunch would be over in ten minutes, but at least she knew exactly what to do when school was out. She had an hour before she had to be at soccer practice, but that should be enough time. Nathan had made it easy. She could fix, test, and push out the upgrade before her mom got there. By the end of the day, she wouldn't have to worry about Click'd sending out personal photos anymore.

She was thinking through the rest of the afternoon, strategizing how to make the change, when Nathan said, "Um . . . Allie. Something's happening." He scooted his chair closer to the monitor and curled his finger toward him. "You have to look at this."

"Now what?"

"I'm not sure." He pointed at the user count in the top right corner of the monitor. "Activity has been steady all through lunch. There were eight hundred and sixty-two users when I sat down, and that barely changed."

"And?"

"It just started spiking. Look." The user base was on the rise again, and it was growing fast.

876.

881.

883.

890.

"Why are you getting all these new users suddenly, especially when the lunch bell is about to ring?"

Nathan's fingers flew across the keyboard. "Here, let me sort it by 'last updated' so we can see the most recent new users. Maybe that will help."

Allie used Nathan's armrest to lean in to get a better

look. She scanned the first twenty names, trying to figure out what they had in common, but she couldn't see a thread. "I don't know any of these people, do you?" she asked, and Nathan shook his head.

"This is so strange," Allie said. "I haven't seen spikes like that since Tuesday, when it first started going around. Why would a bunch of people join out of nowhere?"

They watched the numbers climb:

903.

912.

918.

925.

"That's impossible. There are only nine hundred fourteen students at Mercer."

Nathan's jaw dropped open to say something, but he didn't have a chance to. Allie beat him to it. "Wait. I know her," she said as she pointed to the screen. "She used to be on my soccer team. She goes to Steinbeck." Steinbeck Middle School was two towns away.

The bell rang.

927.

935.

943.

"It's going around Steinbeck." Allie knew she shouldn't see this as good news, but she couldn't help but be a little excited. She shot Nathan a nervous smile.

"Yep." He shook his head and smiled back. "And ten bucks says their lunch just started."

twenty-two

After school, Allie went straight to the lab, and she and Nathan worked together for the next hour. She carefully scrolled through her code, stopping at each line in question, highlighting it, and hitting the DELETE key, carefully separating all connections with the photos app from the other functionality. Every time she pressed DELETE, she thought her heart was going to explode, but she kept going until she reached the last line.

She looked down at the paper Nathan had handed her at lunch, double-checking to be sure she'd followed his handwritten changes perfectly.

Everything matched up.

The leaderboard was no longer connected to the photos in any way. No more ClickPics. No more *woo-hoo*. Allie wondered how long it would take before people noticed.

She took a deep breath and held it as she ran the final test.

"It passed," she told him. She couldn't keep the smile off her face. As much as she hated losing features, she couldn't help but feel relieved.

Her phone chirped by her side and made her jump in her seat.

Mom

In the roundabout

"Are you going to send out the update?" Nathan asked.

"I can't. My mom's here. I have to get to soccer practice." Allie stared at her monitor. "I'll do it when I get home. That way I can run one more test first."

Nathan shook his head. "Send the update, you chicken."

Allie logged out and powered down her computer. "I will. Soon."

He took a big handful of microwave popcorn and stuffed it into his mouth. "You're stalling," he mumbled as he chewed.

She reached for her backpack. "Maybe I am."

■ ■ ■

After soccer practice and dinner, Allie ran up the stairs to her bedroom. She rested her feet on Bo as she sat at her desk working on a math assignment, and then taking an online vocabulary quiz, and finally, reading a chapter on the American Revolution for her social studies class.

By nine o'clock, she still hadn't sent out the update.

"Here goes," she said to herself.

She logged into the CodeGirls server and navigated over to her code. She double-checked all the work she had done in the lab earlier, and pulled Nathan's printout from her backpack to be sure she didn't miss anything. It still matched up perfectly.

Her phone chirped. She picked it up and read the screen:

Nathan

Stop. Stalling.

She laughed quietly. He was right. She'd done everything she could. There was nothing left to do but to send the new version out to the user base.

Allie

I know!!!

OK

I'm doing it right now

She typed up a message to the installed base:

SECURITY UPDATE: REQUIRED INSTALL

Her finger was on the mouse, hovering over the SEND button, ready for her to press it.

Nathan

count of three

Allie took a deep breath and blew it out slowly.

Allie

1

2

Allie pressed SEND.

A few seconds later, the update message showed up on her phone. She installed it and went straight to her profile. Everything looked good. The ultimate test would come in the morning, when people got within range and the photo queue started filling up, but so far, everything seemed to be working.

Allie wanted to keep staring at the screen, but her eyes were burning and she was fighting to keep them open. She tossed the phone on her bed and changed into her pajamas. She was about to go brush her teeth when she heard another *chirp*.

Nathan

you did it

Allie

no YOU did it

WE did it and now we're even

Good luck on Saturday

You too

Goodnight

Allie smiled when she saw the alligator emoji. She was still smiling ten minutes later when she climbed into bed, opened Click'd, and navigated over to the CodeGirls group. Even though it was too late for good day/bad day with Courtney, Allie had to tell her about the good parts.

Allie

1200+ users
fixed the glitch
have more success stories

She put her phone on her nightstand and let her eyes fall shut. As she drifted off, she thought about all the stories she'd gathered so far.

Blake and Jackson. Kira and Sean. Ben and Brody. And then there was Zoe and Ajay, who had been texting each other every night, and Maddie and Chris, who had eaten lunch together that day.

But then she realized she had a sixth one. She thought about the photo she and Nathan took in the lab the day they clicked, and smiled to herself. Their new friendship might have been her favorite story of all.

Friday

twenty-three

≡ Click'd ⚙

Allie Navarro

1214
users

Allie waited on the corner for the bus, feeling exhausted but pumped with adrenaline at the same time.

She couldn't wait to get to school. She was going to try to click with as many people as she could before the first bell rang, and at lunch, she'd make Zoe sneak around with her, finally *playing* the game she'd invented. But most important, she couldn't wait to tell Emma it was fixed. Maybe then she'd reinstall it. Or maybe she never would, and that would be okay, too. She just wanted to make it right for her.

The bus pulled up, the doors slapped open, and Allie climbed the steps with a big grin on her face. But as soon as she hit the landing and she heard Marcus's voice, the smile slipped from her lips.

"What happened, Three?" he asked.

"What do you mean?" she asked. His eyebrows pinched together, and before he could say anything else, she answered her own question. "Oh, the ClickPics? I had to take them down, but don't worry, it's just temporary."

But as she continued to her seat, she realized it wasn't just Marcus. Everyone on the bus was staring at her, and they didn't look happy.

"Where's my leaderboard?" someone called out from the back row.

"Yeah, mine's empty," a girl said.

"They're *all* empty!" another guy added. "Where did everything go?"

What are they talking about? Allie thought as she fell into the seat next to Zoe. "Okay, what's happening?"

"Didn't you open Click'd today?"

"Of course!" Allie immediately responded. It was the first thing she did every morning when she woke up. But then she thought about it.

She'd been curious about the photo queue, so as soon as her alarm sounded, she'd bolted from bed, fired up her computer, and gone straight to the CodeGirls server. She was so thrilled to see it working, her mom had to call her down to breakfast three times, and she'd darted out the door for the bus, speeding to the corner so she wouldn't miss it.

"Actually . . . no. I guess I didn't." She pulled her phone from her pocket and tapped on the icon.

"It's gone?" she said as she stared down at her screen. "Everyone's rankings are gone. What happened?"

"I'm pretty sure that's what everybody on the bus wants to know." Zoe tilted her screen in Allie's direction. It looked the same as hers: nothing but ten question marks next to ten empty photo slots.

Allie's fingers flew across the glass as she opened screen after screen, frantically searching for anything that would help her understand how this could have happened.

"There hasn't been a single *bloop* all morning," Zoe said.

As soon as the bus came to a stop, Allie stepped into the aisle and sprinted down the steps. But she didn't go to her locker. And she didn't go to first-period math, either.

She was heading for the computer lab, but when she turned the corner and spotted the door, there were a bunch of people standing there. She couldn't deal with answering their questions. And she couldn't deal with seeing Ms. Slade. She felt her eyes well up as she took off in the opposite direction. And suddenly, she found herself in front of the library doors.

She ran up the steps to Emma's favorite spot in the corner next to the window, and collapsed into one of the beanbag chairs. She let her face fall into her hands and she sat there, letting the peaceful silence seep into her skin.

The bell rang, but she didn't move.

Her phone chirped, but she ignored it.

She sat there for a long time, going over the events of the night before, thinking about every change she made, every test she ran.

She'd done exactly what Nathan told her to do.

Nathan.

Did he?

No way.

He couldn't have.

She pulled out her phone and started writing a text to him, when the speakers crackled to life and a woman's voice filled the silent library air.

"Allie Navarro, please report to the office. Allie Navarro."

twenty-four

When Allie stepped into the empty hallway, she realized she'd been racing around campus all week—running to the lab, sprinting to her locker, rushing through the lunch lines—but now she wasn't in a hurry at all. She took slow steps, taking as long as she could to get to the office.

She thought about all the teachers Jane had mentioned, and she pictured them lined up outside Mr. Mohr's door, each waiting for a turn to complain about Click'd. She could feel the sweat beading up on her forehead.

She was relieved to find the office empty when she

arrived. "Hi," she said to the assistant behind the counter. "I'm Allie Navarro. Someone paged me?"

"Mr. Mohr had to take a call," she said. And then she pointed to a row of uncomfortable-looking chairs. "Have a seat. It might be a while."

She sat there for a full fifteen minutes, trying not to look as nervous as she felt. Finally, Mr. Mohr's office door opened and he waved her inside.

Allie's heart started racing again, even faster this time. She'd never been inside Mr. Mohr's office. He pointed at a brown leather chair on the other side of his desk and said, "Have a seat, Ms. Navarro."

As Allie sat down, he opened a file on his desk and read it to himself. It was quiet for a long time, and she wished he would say something—anything—because she was starting to feel claustrophobic. And she needed to drown out all the thoughts in her head. She grabbed a chunk of her hair and wrapped it around her finger for something to do with her hands, while she tried to ignore how thick the air in that tiny room felt.

He finally let out a long breath and folded his hands in front of him. "I've been at Mercer Middle School for sixteen years, and I have to tell you, this has probably been the strangest, most interesting first week of school I've ever experienced. Do you know why?"

Allie shook her head.

"Teachers have been complaining all week about classroom disruptions from student phones, and over lunch breaks this week, I've been forced to start confiscating them. We've never had a problem with phones—a few offenders here and there—but for some reason, they've become especially popular all of a sudden."

Allie tried to look like she had no idea what he was talking about.

"Have you heard of an app called Click'd?"

Allie nodded.

"I hadn't heard of it until late yesterday. When I did, I went straight to all the online app stores so I could download it and see how it worked firsthand, but I couldn't find it anywhere." He stood and crossed the room, and then leaned back against the window overlooking the parking lot. "Do you know why I couldn't find it anywhere, Ms. Navarro?" he asked as he folded his arms.

Allie gave him a quick nod.

"It's not in any of the app stores, because Click'd was created by one of our very own students. Isn't that right?"

Allie hugged her chest. She wished she could close her eyes and disappear.

"Tell me about it," he said.

"About Click'd?" Allie asked.

"Yes. Please. What does it do?"

Allie shifted in her seat. "Well, it's an app that helps people find common interests. It learns who you are, and then matches you up with ten people you might want to know."

Mr. Mohr nodded and gave her a half smile. "How did you come up with that idea?"

Allie leaned forward in her seat as she told him all about her summer at CodeGirls camp, and how terrified she was on that first day. "I thought it would be fun to have an app that would help us break the ice," she said. And then she told him all about Courtney, and how she worked next to her for ten weeks, and how the two of them stayed late in the lab, helping each other with their projects and taking turns running out to the vending machine for late-night snacks.

"I worked so hard. I've never worked that hard on anything before. And when I presented to the parents at the end of camp, I got a standing ovation. I've never felt so proud in my whole life. And Ms. Slade was there, and she told me she wanted to mentor me in the Games for Good competition, and . . . I came back for the first day of school walking on air. I couldn't wait to show my friends and my computer science class. And they loved it, too."

Allie realized she was rambling. She stopped and took a few deep breaths.

"I didn't mean to share it. Well, not with that many people . . . It just took off. It started spreading around campus. And on Tuesday, things started going wrong." She told him all about the photo glitch, and how she'd spent the last three days working in the lab and at home each night, trying to figure out how to fix it without breaking anything else.

"Yesterday, Nathan came up with a work-around, just to

get me to the Games for Good competition this weekend. But now . . ." Allie collected herself before she continued. "Now, it doesn't matter anyway. When I fixed the photo glitch, I broke the leaderboard, and the leaderboard is like the heart of the whole thing. And now, I guess . . . it's just . . . over."

She didn't even feel the tears build up. They just started streaming down her cheeks, one after the other. Mr. Mohr handed her a tissue from a box on his desk. She blew her nose and started rambling again.

"Everybody's all annoyed that the app isn't working, but that's not even the point! My *game* isn't *working*! Which means that I don't have *anything* to enter into the contest. And on top of that, my best friend Emma thinks I'm a horrible person, and my friend group is totally falling apart, and all these people I don't even know are fighting with each other, and it's all my fault. Everything's my fault."

When she stopped talking, the room got quiet. Allie wiped her cheeks and blew her nose again.

Mr. Mohr returned to his desk, folded his hands together in front of him, and looked at her. "I can see how hard you've worked and how much this means to you. And I have to say, I'm impressed with your dedication—not only to fixing it, but also to building it in the first place. That's pretty impressive for a twelve-year-old." He laughed to himself. "Actually, that's pretty impressive for *anyone*."

"Thanks," Allie said.

"What has Ms. Slade suggested you do?"

Allie looked down at the carpet. "She doesn't know any of this."

The room got quiet again. "Would you consider telling her?"

Allie felt sick. She didn't want Ms. Slade to know she'd messed up. It was even worse that she'd messed up and hadn't told her when she'd had the chance. But Allie knew Mr. Mohr's question wasn't really a *question* anyway. It was a request. And she didn't have a choice.

"Okay," Allie squeaked out. "I will."

"When do you have computer science class?" he asked.

"Not until sixth period."

"Hmm . . ." He scratched out a note and handed it to her. "Give this to Ms. Slade, please. I'm excusing you from your classes today so you can work with her in the lab and fix your app."

"Really?" Allie looked down at the piece of paper in her hand. And then she looked up at him. "Why?"

He smiled at her. "You spent your summer creating a fun game to help people make friends, and then you spent the whole week in the lab trying to fix it when you learned it was malfunctioning. You didn't have to do that, but you did. That tells me this matters to you. It shows drive and dedication. I think you set a good example for the rest of our students."

Allie couldn't believe what she was hearing, and she couldn't seem to find any words to speak, so she just nodded.

"I could force you to shut your app down, but what kind of message would that send to the rest of the school?"

Allie wanted to hug him, but she didn't. Instead, she stood and said, "Thank you."

"You're welcome."

She gestured toward the door. "I'd better get to work." Allie walked toward it and turned the knob.

"Ms. Navarro," Mr. Mohr said, and Allie stopped and turned to look at him. "Can I ask you one more thing?"

"Sure."

"Why didn't you just shut your game down when you first realized something was wrong?"

It was a good question. She started to give him all the reasons she'd been telling herself all week. That people were having fun. That she needed big numbers for Saturday. That she needed good stories to prove that Click'd was doing good in the world. But as all those answers passed through in her mind, she knew that none of them had anything to do with the real reason she didn't shut it down.

She locked her eyes on Mr. Mohr and told him the truth. "Everyone knew who I was."

twenty-five

Click'd

Allie Navarro

1214
users

"Allie." Ms. Slade looked surprised to see her there. "Everything okay?"

She'd been practicing her speech while she was standing out in the hallway, but now her heart was beating so fast, she wasn't sure she was going to be able to get the whole thing out the way she'd planned.

"No," she began. She took a deep breath, trying to slow her breathing. "Everything's not okay, and I have no idea what to do about it."

She handed her the note from Mr. Mohr. Ms. Slade unfolded it, read it, and then locked her eyes on Allie's. "I think you should start from the beginning."

Allie told her everything. All about the photo glitch and the shared personal pictures and the texts and the fights with her friends. She told her that was why she'd been working so late in the lab—that she wasn't building success stories to add to her presentation like she'd planned to—she was fixing Click'd. She told her about the leaderboard party, and the underwear shot, and the photos she'd missed, and the fights she'd overheard on campus.

"Nathan thought he knew how to fix it. And when he told me about an issue he was having with Built, I thought I could help him, too. So we switched stations. I came through for him, but last night, when I made the changes he suggested, it somehow disconnected the leaderboard."

Allie was trying not to sound accusatory, but she couldn't help it. She thought back to the events of the day before. Nathan had highlighted everything she needed to change, but she had made the changes herself. And she'd tested it all, countless times. She couldn't imagine he'd do anything to hurt her on purpose, but given that he had a working app and she no longer did, she couldn't ignore the possibility.

She thought about Nathan, sitting next to her with his headphones on. Had he only installed the app because he was trying to get a look inside? Maybe he was trying to sabotage her from the beginning. He knew she had a chance at beating him this time, so he'd decided there was no way he was going to let that happen.

But then she thought about all their lunches in the lab,

reaching into the popcorn bag as they worked on their code, and texting each other as they stayed up late, troubleshooting from home. Had he been playing her all along? She didn't want to think it was possible.

Ms. Slade curled her finger toward her chest and led Allie to the back of the room. Allie fired up her computer while Ms. Slade sat in Nathan's seat.

"Remember, it's my job to help you find the problem and do whatever I need to do to help you solve it, but I'm a mentor. I can't fix it for you."

Allie nodded. That wasn't news; she knew the G4G rules.

"Okay, let's take a look and see if we can figure out what's going on," Ms. Slade said. The classroom started filling up with her second-period class, but she didn't leave Allie's side.

She logged into the CodeGirls server and went straight to the cloud-based database. Allie scrolled down slowly, one line at a time. The answers to everyone's questions were still there, and she stared at them, trying not to cry. Everything looked right. The algorithm that gathered each person's leaderboard data and ranked it against the others in the system seemed to be working exactly the way it was supposed to.

"I have a backup," Allie said. "I could just revert back to the old code and everything will return to the way it was last night."

Ms. Slade's eyebrows shot up. "But then Click'd would

go back to randomly pulling pictures from people's private photos?"

"Yeah." Allie felt guilty for not caring, but what was the worst that could happen? It was Friday. As soon as she got it running again, she could take it offline for the rest of the day.

"The judges would never figure something like that out, Allie. But you would know. And I would know." She pointed at the monitor. "I'm afraid you're going to need to fix it, for real this time."

Allie looked at her teacher. A big part of her wished she'd never told Ms. Slade the truth. Why didn't she just go straight to Ira, revert to the code before she made the changes, and send out another update to the user base? It was that easy to get the leaderboard running again. And then everyone would be happy.

But she knew deep down that would have been wrong.

She stood up and paced the room. She couldn't bring herself to look at the screen. She had over 1,200 users, but none of it mattered without a working leaderboard. If she couldn't fix it by the end of the day, she would have to use the CodeGirls group as the example in her demo.

And that's when she had a horrible thought.

"No," she whispered.

She reached for her phone, opened Click'd, and switched over to the CodeGirls group. She clicked on "leaderboard" and her heart sank deep in her chest.

It was empty, too.

Her CodeGirls were gone. Wiped out. All of them.

Courtney lived in Arizona. Kaiya was back in Boston. Alexa was in Georgia, Maya was in Denver, Zaina was in Chicago, Rachel was in Florida, Li was in Texas, Layla was in Oregon, Shonna was in Illinois, and Jayne lived in North Carolina. Seeing those ten names on her leaderboard, knowing they would always be there because her CodeGirls leaderboard would never change, made her feel connected to them, even though they were far away. She remembered the day they'd run around the lab, tapping phones and watching their leaderboards come together. She could never re-create that moment. And without the phone tap, she wasn't sure she could even re-create the leaderboard itself.

The bell rang and Ms. Slade rested her hand on Allie's back. "Hey, it's okay. Remember, it's code. It's inherently fixable."

Allie folded her hands on the desk and let her head fall.

Last night, for a brief time, she had a working app *without* a photo glitch, more than a thousand users, and tons of data. But two empty leaderboards meant she had nothing to show the judges the following day. It might be fixable, but she had no idea how she was going to figure it out in less than twenty-four hours.

"My app relies on the leaderboard. Even if I'm able to find the problem and fix the code, how am I going to re-create a leaderboard by tomorrow?"

Ms. Slade was quiet while she studied Allie's screen.

"May I?" she asked, and when Allie nodded, she reached for the mouse.

"Hmm . . ." she said as she looked over all the information in the various database tables. Allie watched her work, trying not to jump out of her seat and run back to the quiet corner in the library. She thought about those colorful beanbag chairs and the way the light streamed in through the tall windows.

"Well, as far as I can tell, you have two problems to solve. First, you need to figure out what's wrong with the algorithm that ties everything to the leaderboard. And once you figure it out—which I *know* you can do—you need to create a new leaderboard filled with people you can physically locate. A bunch of your users don't even go to school here."

Allie groaned. She knew she was right.

"I have an idea, but I don't think you're going to like it. What if you delete all your users and start from scratch?"

Allie's head snapped up. "What?"

"Well, not delete," Ms. Slade explained. "Just unflag every record for now, so you can start clean and work with a smaller user base. You can always re-flag everyone when it's fixed and the competition is done."

"But I added over a *thousand* users this week! That's huge. You said it yourself, the judges look for things like that."

"And that's true, but they also look for working apps," Ms. Slade said plainly.

Allie put her elbows on the desk and dropped her head

in her hands, and Ms. Slade scooted in closer and rested her hand on Allie's shoulder.

"It's not the end of the world! You'll get all those users back in no time. Just remember, you were selected for the Games for Good competition based entirely on your CodeGirls summer project, back when you had twenty users and an incredible story to tell. Focus on that. And keep in mind, you had an extraordinary week. There was pure *enthusiasm* in every corner of this campus. For *your* game, Allie. For this thing that didn't even exist three months ago—not until you used your imagination to create it, and your skill and passion to bring it to life. *You* did that." She squeezed her hand hard. "You."

Allie wanted to cry, but she nodded instead.

"I think Mr. Mohr is the only one who *wasn't* excited about it." Ms. Slade joked, and Allie couldn't help but smile. "And based on that note he just wrote, you even made him come around. You took your app through the most brutal beta test imaginable, and it passed with flying colors."

Allie laughed. "How can you even say that?" she asked as she held up her phone, touched her icon, launched it, and watched it crash.

Ms. Slade raised an eyebrow. And then she looked at Allie and played with her earrings. One was a little wrench. The other was a tiny hammer. "You have all the tools you need to fix this. And after you knock those judges' socks off tomorrow, you can get all those users back."

Allie pictured unflagging all twelve-hundred-plus

names. She wouldn't have to worry about losing any of the data, and she could focus on a smaller, more manageable sample size. She was basically starting from scratch, like she did over the summer with the CodeGirls.

"Okay," Allie whispered.

Ms. Slade snapped her fingers. "Hey, and if you can get the code fixed by the end of lunch, you can make our advanced CS class your user base. Their profiles and answers are already in the system. Just flag them when you're ready, and as soon as they walk into class, you can start matching. Your leaderboard will be back up and running by the end of sixth period."

It was a good solution. So why did it make her feel like such a failure?

Allie sighed. "I'll be right back where I was on Monday."

"Was Monday so bad?" Ms. Slade asked.

Allie remembered sitting with Maddie, Emma, and Zoe on the little path between the garden and the science building, watching over their shoulders as they each took the quiz. She pictured the four of them running around campus, listening for *bloops*, watching for clues, and trying to find one another. She remembered how the four of them clicked on the staircase by the gym, and the *woo-hoo* sound that told them to snap a selfie together. Allie thought about the look in their eyes when they told her how much they loved her game.

"No," Allie said. "Actually, Monday was really good."

twenty-six

Allie didn't move when the lunch bell rang.

"Ms. Navarro," Ms. Slade said. "You've been sitting in that same spot for almost four hours."

"Yeah," Allie said without taking her eyes off her screen.

"Get up, please. Go outside. Say hello to your friends. Get some food."

"I'm not hungry." As Allie said the words, she felt her stomach grumble.

"Go. Now." Ms. Slade leaned over her shoulder and picked up the mouse. Allie didn't even realize she'd done it until she reached out to use it and it wasn't there.

Allie let out a heavy sigh. "Fine," she mumbled as she

scooted away from her desk. "I'll be back in ten."

She stepped into the hallway and took a deep breath, pulling the late summer air deep into her lungs. She walked quickly toward the quad, taking the long way and avoiding the busier routes. When people spotted her, she ducked into the closest bathroom, or turned toward a wall and pretended to look for something in her backpack. It took longer than it should have, but she finally reached the lunch line, and when she did, she stood with her head low, hoping no one would notice her. She couldn't wait to get back to the lab, where she could put on her headphones and focus on her code again.

Allie took her sandwich to go. When she opened the computer lab door, Nathan was standing at Ms. Slade's desk.

She stared at him.

"I'm just filling Nathan in," Ms. Slade said.

Allie bit down hard on her lip. "Did you know?" she asked him.

"Know what?"

"That disconnecting ClickPics would wipe out the leaderboard."

"No, of course not."

"But you said you tested it."

"I did. You tested it, too."

"Just to be sure it was completely disconnected from the photos app. You said you tested it against the leaderboard a bunch of times, and I believed you."

"I did."

"Then why don't I have a working app, Nathan?" she yelled.

Allie stared at him. She could feel her eyes narrowing.

"I didn't do this on purpose," he said.

"How am I supposed to know that?" Allie bit the inside of her cheek to keep from crying. She couldn't cry. If she did, Nathan would think she was sad, and she wasn't sad. She was angry. She was angrier than she'd been in her whole life.

"Because I—"

Allie cut him off. "Because you couldn't stand the idea of losing to me." Allie looked at Ms. Slade. "I *trusted* him. And he trusted me. Only I didn't let him down." And then she turned back to Nathan. "By the way, how is the hardware store working out for you? Everybody still being charged for paint?"

Nathan didn't say a word. He looked down at the ground and shook his head. "I was trying to help," he said to Allie. And then he looked at Ms. Slade. "I worked on her code for hours. I tested it on Wednesday night and again in the lab, and it was working just fine."

"Except it isn't fine," Allie said.

"Do you really think he sabotaged your game?" Ms. Slade asked.

Years of anger and frustration bubbled up inside Allie. She'd lost to him too many times. And she'd seen that smug look on his face after every one. She thought this time would be different, but she was beginning to realize she was wrong.

"I don't know," she said calmly. "But we're less than twenty-four hours away from the biggest competition of our lives, and he has a working game, and I don't. I think that's kind of hard to ignore, don't you?"

Nathan shook his head. He wasn't about to take the blame. "Did you write the last line exactly the way I said to? Because that was what tied it all back to the leaderboard."

"Of course I did," Allie said. She couldn't even look at him.

"You followed his instructions exactly?" Ms. Slade asked. "You didn't change anything else?"

"No."

"You must have missed something," Nathan said.

Allie narrowed her eyes on him. "I didn't."

"Where's the printout I gave you?"

"In my backpack."

"Great. Let's get it. I'll help you fix it, right now." Nathan pointed to Ira.

Allie laughed loudly. "Are you kidding? I'm not letting you anywhere near my code!" Nathan still looked confused and hurt, but that didn't keep her from getting right in his face. "Excuse me. I have a ton of work to do and no time to do it."

She turned on her heel and walked away. She sat down in front of her computer, pulled her headphones over her ears, and turned her music up as loud as it would go.

twenty-seven

Right before fifth period, Ms. Slade walked to the back of the room and sat down next to Allie. "How's it going?"

Allie looked up at the clock. There was no way she'd have everything done in time to make her sixth-period class into her new installed base.

"It failed the last test. I'm pretty sure I know what to do next, but I still have to test everything again."

"That's okay," Ms. Slade said calmly. "We'll just need to find another concentrated group of people you can reach before the day is over. What other options do you have?"

Allie thought about it. Emma, Zoe, and Maddie could

meet her after school, but that would only get her three people on her leaderboard. She wouldn't see her soccer team until their game on Sunday. She could call a leaderboard party on the blacktop, but that was too risky. And besides, she didn't want to stay after school. She couldn't wait to get home. She was counting the minutes until the bus pulled up in front of her house and the doors slapped open.

The bus.

That was it.

"There are probably thirty people on my bus," she told Ms. Slade. "And they've all joined this week, so I already have all their information in the database."

"Perfect," Ms. Slade said, patting her hand. "As Captain Picard says—"

"Make it so," Allie said, finishing Ms. Slade's sentence. Everyone knew it was her favorite Star Trek line. Allie didn't even need to turn her head and look at the poster on the wall behind her.

"Attagirl," she said as she left Allie alone with her code and walked back to the front of the room to teach her next class.

Allie worked all through fifth period and into sixth. By the time seventh period was about to start, all her tests had passed and she was ready to push out the update.

She checked the calculations. She made certain there weren't any mistakes. Everything looked solid, so she flagged the database table with everyone that rode Bus #14.

If she'd done everything right, the drive home would be full of *bloops* and taps and flying phones. It would be just like that day in the Fishbowl with her CodeGirls. Everyone's leaderboards would be full in a matter of minutes.

Zoe would be #1. Marcus would be her #6. Penny would be #7. It would all fall into place, exactly the way it had earlier that week.

Right before the final bell was about to ring, Ms. Slade returned.

"I'm sending out the update," Allie told her. But she couldn't quite bring herself to press the button. She kept staring at the code, wondering if she was missing anything.

"You should be so proud of yourself," Ms. Slade said.

Allie smiled. "I will be if it works."

Ms. Slade smiled back. "You should be, even if it doesn't."

Allie combed her fingers through her hair. She didn't want to ask the question that had been running through her mind all day, but she didn't have a choice. "What happens if . . . if it doesn't work? Do I have to drop out?"

Ms. Slade nodded. "I'm afraid so. But you can be in the Games for Good Pavilion."

Allie brought her elbows to the table and rested her chin in her hands. She'd been so focused on the stage presentation, she'd forgotten all about the Games for Good Pavilion. Now she pictured a kiosk with her beautiful logo on a sign above a bright monitor, and her stomach clenched into a tight knot.

Ms. Slade reached for Allie's spiral-bound notebook and wrote something on the first page. Then she slid it back to her. "That's my cell phone. Call or text me and let me know what's going on. It doesn't matter what time it is."

"Thanks," she said. And then Allie pushed the UPDATE button, reactivating Click'd for all the people on Bus #14.

twenty-eight

Click'd

Allie Navarro

1
user

At the end of the day, Allie ran straight to the office. As promised, there was a packet waiting for her on the counter with a Post-it note on top that read *Assignments for Allie Navarro*. She quickly scanned the contents, raced to her locker to grab the books she needed, and took off for the roundabout, texting Zoe on the way:

Allie

meet me on the lawn by the bus

need your help!

She ran as fast as she could, feeling her backpack thump against her spine with every step.

Allie couldn't help noticing that everything was different. No one was racing through the halls, trying to locate a match. People weren't tapping their phones in the air or squealing with delight as they looked at their newly posted leaderboards. No one was taking ClickPics. And she didn't hear a single *bloop*.

She pushed her way through the crowd, ignoring everyone as they tried to stop her with questions about Click'd.

"What happened?"

"I heard it would be back up by the time school got out!"

"Where is it?"

As she turned at the flagpole, she spotted Zoe up ahead. She took off sprinting and didn't stop until she was standing in front of her, panting.

Allie told her about fixing the glitch and rewriting the code. "It's all up and running, but this thirty-minute bus ride is my last chance to fill up my leaderboard for the contest tomorrow."

"What do you need me to do?" Zoe asked, and Allie wanted to hug her.

"Open Click'd."

The two of them started walking toward the bus while Zoe pulled out her phone and tapped her finger against the glass. As soon as Allie reached the top step, she heard *bloop-bloop-bloop*.

Zoe's phone let out the same sound.

Allie smiled and held her phone out, and Zoe did the same. When they tapped them together, their leaderboards popped up on their screens.

Allie stood at the front of the bus. It was almost completely full. People were turned around in their seats, talking to one another.

"Hi!" she called out. "Can I have your attention, please?" The noise level gradually dropped, and soon, everyone was staring at her.

"Hi," Allie repeated nervously. "So . . . hey . . . I need a favor." She fidgeted with her hands, wringing them in front of her. "I just released an update of Click'd, but I only sent it to you guys—to everyone on bus fourteen." She briefly explained what happened with the photos and how she'd fixed the glitch but lost the leaderboard and had to start from scratch. "In order to participate in tomorrow's Games for Good competition, I need a working leaderboard and at least twenty members. And that's where all of you come in. I need you to be my beta testers for the new version. Please don't invite anyone else to join yet—they can't anyway, because they aren't in the system anymore." Her gaze traveled around the bus and she met eyes with a few people. "You guys in?" she said, giving them a hopeful smile.

"Sure," someone in the back yelled.

"Of course," Penny said.

"What do we need to do?" Marcus asked from his spot in the third row.

Allie smiled at him, and then she addressed the group again. "Just launch Click'd and it will prompt you to install the update."

Marcus reached for his phone and everyone else on the bus did the same. Zoe and Allie walked to their seats and sat down.

Every time a new person stepped on the bus, someone nearby explained what was happening, and soon everyone had downloaded the update and the *bloop-bloop-bloops* began flying as screens flashed red. People tapped their phones together and watched as their leaderboards changed before their eyes.

Allie's leaderboard was half-full before the bus even left the roundabout, and so was Zoe's. The energy level inside was sky-high as everyone passed their phones around—just like they'd done earlier that week—laughing and joking as they tapped them together and admired their new leaderboards. Nobody appeared to care that the *woo-hoo* sound was gone or that the ClickPics feature had been disabled.

"You did it," Zoe said.

Allie was beaming as she relaxed back into the seat.

She closed her eyes and listened to the *bloops*. She smiled when she heard people yelling, "Yes!" and shouting out their ranking. People hugged and high-fived. And it all felt fun again.

She looked around, thinking about how strange it was that thirty-two kids in three different grades, who were trapped on a bus for forty-five minutes, twice each day, usually rode in silence, barely speaking to each other, but now, they were all becoming friends—and it was all because of Click'd.

It was the kind of story the judges would want to hear.

Allie stood and started taking pictures, eager to try to capture the energy of the moment so she could weave it into her presentation as soon as she got home.

But then she heard a voice from the back of the bus. "What happened?"

"Uh-oh," another voice said.

Allie looked down at her phone. Click'd had crashed.

"Launch it again!" Allie called out.

She navigated over to the main screen and touched her fingertip to the icon. Click'd launched and her profile filled the screen. It stayed like that for a few seconds. She waited for a sound. Or a vibration. *Anything.*

All the phones were silent again. No *bloops*. No flashing screens. No picture clues. No leaderboard.

Allie tapped the icon again. Her profile opened. But when she opened the leaderboard tab, the whole thing crashed again.

"No." She stared at the screen. She shut down her phone and started it up again. She launched Click'd again. That time, it didn't even open her profile before it crashed.

Allie wanted to scream. Or cry. Or hit something hard. She pictured herself doing all three at the same time as soon as she got home.

"It's okay," Zoe said reassuringly. "You can fix it. The leaderboards are full now and you've got thirty-two users."

But Allie couldn't speak. When the bus stopped at her corner, she still hadn't said a word. Before she stood up, Zoe took her face in her hands and squeezed her cheeks. "Look at me. You're going to go inside, run your tests, or whatever it is you do, and figure it out, okay?"

Allie tried to smile, but she couldn't. Zoe was squeezing her face too hard.

"Text me as soon as you fix it," Zoe said, and she let her hands drop.

Allie stood and walked down the aisle in a haze. As she passed Marcus, he said, "Hey, I'm sorry, Three."

Allie blew out a breath. "Me too, Six."

twenty-nine

Allie's mom tapped her fingernails against the table. "Please make your phone stop," she said.

Buzz.

Buzz.

Buzz.

It had been like that ever since she left school that afternoon. One text after another, each one saying pretty much the same thing:

Did you know
Click'd isn't working?!?

> I keep clicking the icon
> but nothing happens!

> Are you fixing it?

> When will it be up again???

Allie pushed her chair away from the table and walked into the kitchen with Bo on her heels. She turned her phone off before she set it on the counter. She didn't want to hear it or see it. She just wanted everyone to leave her alone.

She returned to her chair and took a slice of pepperoni pizza from the box in the center of the table. Bo settled back into his usual spot right under her feet, and Allie dug her toes into his soft fur. She wished she could hide under the table, too. It seemed quiet down there.

"You okay?" her dad asked.

Allie shook her head.

"You might feel better if you talk to us about it," he added.

"I don't need to talk about it." Allie took a big bite and washed it down with her milk. "But you know what I do need?" she asked sarcastically. "A working app. Do either of you happen to have one of those?"

Her parents were silent.

Maybe I don't need a working app, Allie thought. *Maybe I don't deserve to be there after all.*

Click'd had been a total failure. It had caused fights all over the school, embarrassed people in ways she'd never be able to apologize for, and it almost ruined her friendship with Emma.

She had no business being in the Games for Good competition. Clearly, Click'd wasn't *good*.

"Is there anything we can do to help?" her mom asked.

Allie took another bite and chewed while she thought about it. "I don't know. Maybe. I'm going to spend the next few hours trying to figure out why it's crashing, and . . ." She trailed off. She didn't know how to finish the sentence.

"Maybe you're closer than you think?" Her dad tried to sound positive. "You fixed the big stuff, right? It was working on the bus. You just have some stability issues, that's all." He made it sound like it was so easy, but Allie knew it wasn't.

She stared at her food. She knew she needed to go back to her room, back to that desk, and back to those never-ending lines of code, but she was so tired of looking at them. She just wanted to sit in front of the TV, eating popcorn and watching a movie like the three of them did every Friday night.

Popcorn. That reminded her of her week in the lab. She thought about Nathan and got angry all over again.

"Do you have a plan B? Just in case?" Allie's mom asked.

"There's no plan B," Allie said. If she couldn't keep Click'd from crashing, she would have to withdraw from the competition. "No working code, nothing to enter."

"Well, that's only half-true," her mom said. "You're supposed to be demo-ing in the pavilion all day, too. You have to show up."

Ugh. Not the pavilion again, she thought.

"No way. If I can't fix Click'd, the Games for Good Pavilion will have to have one empty kiosk." She pushed her pizza away. "I'm not going. Not a chance." Just thinking about being on that exhibit floor without a fully functional, amazing-looking app made her feel nauseated.

"Well, even if you can't be in the competition, you still need to be in the pavilion."

Allie let out a sarcastic laugh. "What am I supposed to do, Mom? Stand there while people stare at a screenshot of a broken app? People are coming to the conference to see games. I can't be there if I don't have one to show them."

"But you have a game to talk about," her dad suggested.

"No one cares about that," Allie said.

The room fell silent. Nobody said anything for almost a full minute. Allie was about to go back to her room when her dad spoke up.

"You know that demo you did at CodeGirls Camp last weekend?"

Allie rolled her eyes. "Yeah."

"Do you know what part I loved most?"

Allie pictured the voting app. She thought about the two people with the blue screens, who walked from opposite sides of the auditorium. She thought about the moment Courtney joined her onstage.

"The part where I didn't suck?" Allie asked.

Her dad ignored her sarcastic tone. "The part I loved most was when you showed all those pictures of you and the rest of the girls in the lab, and told stories about how you became friends."

He leaned forward on the table and she found herself doing the same.

"That's when everybody in that auditorium got goose bumps. It wasn't because of your app; it was because of the experience you had. You talked about being afraid in a room full of strangers, and you talked about all the CodeGirls getting to know things about one another they never would have learned without Click'd. That was the most powerful part of your presentation—the stories you told."

Allie's ears perked up. "Seriously? *That* was the best part?"

Her dad looked at her mom, and her mom nodded along with him.

Allie thought about that. She had pictures. And she had plenty of stories. She was planning to pull a bunch of ClickPics into her presentation, anyway. It wouldn't take long to turn them into a slideshow.

"It's still plan B," her mom said. "But it's better than nothing."

She couldn't stand the idea of giving up, and she wasn't about to—not yet—but if she couldn't fix it, at least she'd have something to show people when they came to the booth.

And she knew Ms. Slade expected her to be there, with or without a working app.

"I'd better get back to work," she said with a sigh. She took another slice of pizza to go and trudged up the stairs with Bo right on her heels.

Back in her room, she opened her code again and started from the beginning. She tweaked a few things and then tested it. And it failed. She tweaked and tested again, and it failed again. She pored over every detail, line after line, trying to figure out what was making it crash.

"What am I missing?" she asked herself.

And then she started from the top and scrolled down, studying every connection to every database table again.

Just after midnight, she thought she found the problem in a line that was somehow calling the same table twice. She deleted one instance, and was about to run another test when she changed her mind. At that point, she figured the test didn't even matter. No one else was awake anyway. It would either work or it wouldn't.

Last chance, she thought as she executed the program.

And then she held her breath.

She reached for her phone and tapped on the icon.

Click'd launched exactly the way it was supposed to. And suddenly, she was staring at her profile.

"It works," she said. Bo stood when he heard her voice and started wagging his tail excitedly. She looked down at him, beaming. "It works."

It was *actually* working.

She couldn't believe it was *actually* working.

She clicked on the leaderboard and braced herself, waiting for it to crash. But it didn't.

She clicked on Zoe's profile picture. She clicked on

Lauren's. And then Penny's. She was just about to click on Marcus's when the screen went dark.

"No . . ." she groaned as she collapsed back into her chair. She stared at her phone, and then back at the code, and then back at her phone again. There was no getting around it. Tears welled up in her eyes as she glanced at the time: 12:24 a.m.

As the tears slipped down her cheeks, she typed a message to Ms. Slade:

Allie

> Please pull my name from G4G

Saturday

thirty

Allie and her parents stood at the top of the escalator, looking down onto the show floor.

"There it is," her dad said. But Allie had already seen the Games for Good Pavilion. It was huge, and the fact that it was bright blue and white, smack in the middle of the show floor, and surrounded by dark-colored gaming booths, made it impossible to miss.

She felt her mom's arm on her back. "Are you okay?"

"Yeah," Allie said, even though it wasn't true. She already wanted to cry, and she had no idea how she was going to get through the day without doing it.

Her dad rested a supportive hand on her back. "I know

this isn't at all what you expected out of today, but we are so proud of you. You know that, right?"

Allie shut her eyes and nodded quickly. And then she grabbed a chunk of her hair and twirled it around her finger. She stared down at the pavilion again, knowing that just inside, there was a small kiosk with her Click'd logo on it.

"Go down there and tell everyone about your game," her mom said. "Don't think about what went wrong. Don't think about the fact that you're not in the competition. Just focus on everything that went right. Tell your stories."

Allie nodded. *And don't think about Nathan,* she thought. *Don't even look at his kiosk. Don't even think about what he did.*

"Remember: twelve hundred users in three days," her dad said.

"Twelve hundred and fourteen," her mom said, correcting him.

Allie forced a smile. "Including Taylor Swift."

"Exactly! See, now that's a good story." Her mom grabbed her shoulders with both hands and pivoted her toward the escalator. "Come on. Let's go have some fun."

They followed the crowd into the exhibit hall and flashed their badges for the security guard. Inside, there were people everywhere, racing around, putting the final touches on their booth displays. They were testing microphones and loading their games on giant screens. Huge signs hovered in the air, advertising a bunch of games she had on her phone and more she'd never even heard of.

As soon as Allie and her parents stepped onto the bright white carpet, a woman in ripped jeans, black Converse, and a bright blue T-shirt that read *G4G Pavilion Coordinator* came up and introduced herself. "Hi," she said, extending her hand toward Allie. "I'm Jen." She shook hands with her parents. "Follow me."

She led them over to a kiosk, and Allie's breath hitched when she saw her sign. Click'd was in big block print above her logo. She looked at it and felt the corners of her mouth turn up. She still loved the pencil-thin swirls that formed two stick figures with their arms around each other.

"You should have everything here: cables, connectors, keyboard, touchpad," Jen said brightly as she pointed to each item on the narrow shelf. "But give a shout if there's anything else you need, okay?" She checked her watch. "The show floor opens in forty minutes. You good?"

Allie was wondering if Jen knew that she wouldn't be up on the stage like the rest of the people in the pavilion. She was about to ask her when Jen stepped forward, closing the distance between them.

"Hey," she said. "I'm sorry about your game." Allie bit down on the inside of her cheek. "I've made special arrangements for you to sit next to your guests in the audience. Your badge will get you in a little early. Look for the seats in the front row with your names on them."

Allie dipped her chin to her chest and stared at the stark white carpet.

Jen squeezed in closer. "It happens all the time, you know?"

She looked up. "It does?"

"Yep," she said. "Almost every year, there's someone in the pavilion who had to drop out of the formal competition. And it's okay. Your app will still go up on our website whenever it's ready, and you'll get to tell a ton of people about it today. So try to have fun, okay? You've earned this spot." She pointed up at the sign above their heads. "I can't wait to play your game. It sounds amazing."

"It is." Allie heard Ms. Slade's voice from behind her, and she slowly turned around. She found her teacher standing there in a light blue suit with a crisp white shirt. She was wearing more makeup than she typically wore in class, and her hair was even curlier than usual. Allie thought she looked beautiful.

"Hi," Allie said as she tried to swallow down the giant lump in her throat.

Ms. Slade reached out and took Allie's hand in hers, gripping it hard. "Allie . . . I'm kind of at a loss for words today. I'm so sorry. But at the same time, I'm so proud of you."

"For what?" The words squeaked out of Allie's mouth.

"For . . . everything. For building your app. For working all week to fix it. For being here in the pavilion. I've never been so proud of one of my students."

Allie forced a smile. She tried to say thank you, but nothing came out.

"Here," Ms. Slade said. "These are for you." She pressed a small box into Allie's hands.

Allie opened it, and inside, she found a pair of dangly Click'd logo earrings, just like the ones Ms. Slade had worn to the CodeGirls demo a week earlier. She looked up to thank her, and realized Ms. Slade was wearing one in her left ear, too. And in her right, she wore one of the little houses from Built.

"I'm going to go check on Nathan. Let me know if you need anything, okay?"

Nathan.

Allie watched her walk away until she reached Nathan's kiosk. He was on the opposite side of the pavilion, and Allie realized for the first time that she had an unobstructed view. His sign looked perfect: two of his animated characters were leaning against either side of a colorful house with the word BUILT forming the roof.

Nathan was wearing a pair of khaki shorts, tennis shoes, and a black throwback T-shirt with an Atari logo on the front. She could see his monitor and the small neighborhood street, complete with miniature cars and trees lining the sidewalks, and those little characters standing on tall ladders with their hammers in hand, pounding away on the side of a tiny house.

Then he turned his head and caught Allie looking at him. He held up his hand, giving her a small wave, but she didn't return it. Instead, she turned her back to him and kept setting up her slideshow.

When the show floor opened at ten o'clock, the exhibit hall came to life as it filled with people. It got louder and louder as games from neighboring booths competed with one another for attention. There were games running on oversize screens designed to look like phones, and movie theater–size screens with huge groups of people gathered around them. Off to one side, Allie spotted a bunch of people standing in line to take turns jumping up in the air in front of a green screen while a photographer snapped a picture, converted them into animated characters, and placed them into a game setting.

"Hi." Allie looked down when she heard the voice, and saw a young girl standing next to her. She was watching the pictures on Allie's screen.

"What's your game?" the little girl asked, pointing up at the sign.

"It's called Click'd. I created it to help people make new friends."

"That sounds fun," the girl said.

Allie looked over at her monitor right as the picture changed to one of her and Courtney. The slideshow continued, slowly rolling through all the pictures people had taken over the last few days and all the ClickPics from the leaderboard party. But Allie's favorites were the shots of her real-life best friends, taken on the staircase on the first day of school.

"My friend Zoe may have had the most fun." Allie pointed to the picture of Zoe, racing across the lawn with her arm in the air and a huge smile on her face. And then she leaned down like she was telling the girl a secret. "She got a little bit carried away," she said as she crinkled her nose and let out a laugh. The little girl copied her expression and laughed along.

The next picture was the ClickPic Maddie and Chris took that day in the quad. "And my friend Maddie actually started talking to this boy she's liked for a whole year."

The next photo filled the screen. It was Allie and Emma on the stairs with their arms around each other. "And my friend Emma . . ." She didn't know how to finish her sentence. "Well, let's just say that Emma wasn't such a big fan of my game," she finally said. "But I click with her in real life, and that's all that really matters." Allie wished she had realized that earlier. Clicking with Emma in real life was always the most important thing.

The little girl smiled up at her. "I built a game at school. It's called Tiger Run. Because I love tigers. I'd show it to you, but I don't have it on my phone."

"Darn. I wish I could see that." Allie smiled at her. "What grade are you in?"

"Fourth."

"Hey, that's how old I was when I started coding." Allie gave her a high five. And then she curled her finger toward her chest. "Want to see the code?" she asked, and the girl's eyes lit up as she stepped in closer and came up on her tiptoes.

thirty-one

"Attention, everyone! The Fourth Annual Games for Good Competition is starting in fifteen minutes in Theater A."

Allie squeezed her eyelids tight and gripped the sides of her kiosk with both hands.

"Ready?" She heard her dad's voice behind her, but she didn't turn around. She didn't open her eyes. She didn't loosen her grip.

"I think I'll wait here," she said.

"Allie . . ." It was her mom's voice that time.

But she shook her head slowly. "I can't do it, Mom."

"What if we told you we had a surprise for you?" her dad said.

Allie opened her eyes and stared at one of the signs hanging from the ceiling. She blew out a breath. "What is it?"

"Well, it wouldn't be a surprise if we told you, would it? Come on," he said as he led her out of the pavilion and toward the exhibit-hall exit.

When they reached Theater A, a man at the front door handed her a program and said, "Welcome. Do you need help finding your seats?"

"No, thank you," her dad said. "We know where we're going."

They stepped inside, and she followed her parents to the first row. The music was loud and upbeat. Allie tipped her chin back and counted ten gigantic screens hanging from the ceiling, all placed at key points so everyone could see them. And the room was enormous—filled with seats in neat rows, all facing a circular stage in the center—and already packed with people.

When they arrived at their seats, Allie's jaw dropped. Emma, Zoe, and Maddie were sitting in the front row, and as soon as they saw her, they jumped up and wrapped their arms around her.

"What are you doing here? You shouldn't have come," Allie said.

"We told you we'd be here!" Zoe said.

"To watch me compete, but now . . ." Allie trailed off. She couldn't finish her sentence.

"We wanted to be here," Maddie said.

"Yeah, I wasn't about to miss this nerd party," Zoe said as she craned her neck and looked around the room. "This place is *ah-maze-ing!*"

Emma didn't say anything at first. She stared at Allie. "It's my fault, isn't it?"

Allie rested her hand on her friend's shoulder. "No, it's not."

"You were right. You should have left the code alone. If I hadn't insisted you fix it—" Emma began, but Maddie cut her off.

"No, it's my fault," she said. "It was my idea for you to share it in the first place. You wanted to wait until the competition was over. I should have listened to you."

"It's not your fault," Allie said to Maddie. And then she looked at Emma. "And it's not your fault, either. It was one hundred percent mine. I shared it because I got worried about Nathan's game. I got competitive. If I'd shut it down as soon as I realized it was sharing personal pics, I would have been up on that stage, introducing Click'd and its more than three hundred users. Instead, I'm here in the audience, watching."

Allie's gaze traveled up to the stage and hung there, taking in the lights and the huge projection screen, and it was all she could do not to cry.

She was relieved when the houselights dimmed, the music went silent, and everyone took their seats. A spotlight shined on the stage, and when Allie looked up, she saw the Spyglass CEO, Naomi Ryan, standing right in the center.

"Welcome! Thank you all for coming to the Fourth Annual Games for Good Youth Developers Competition." When the applause died down and people returned to their seats, she began pacing the stage slowly.

"I created Spyglass to entertain people. I built this company to bring fun, unique, expertly designed, slick-looking games to mobile devices. I'm excited to say we've achieved that, thanks to our hardworking developers and to all the partners we have in this room. But if you know me, you know this: I never intended to stop there. We're all here for a bigger reason: to use our collective talents to make this world better than we found it."

The room exploded into applause.

She smiled as she clapped along and paced the stage, waiting for the room to quiet down.

"Today you're going to meet nine passionate developers. The youngest one is twelve years old. The oldest just turned nineteen. These games are planting trees, protecting endangered animals, teaching people how to survive a massive pandemic, providing bicycles for people in impoverished villages, and grooming people to be teachers in countries where girls are not allowed to learn."

Allie felt goose bumps travel up her arms.

Naomi Ryan walked to the front of the stage and stood

there quietly, waiting for the applause to die down before she continued.

"I promise, you will leave this room today feeling inspired and enlightened. I promise that you will leave this room feeling devastated, because only one person can win this year's Games for Good competition. And I promise you will leave this room today with renewed hope for the future of this planet, because you're about to meet representatives of a generation that thinks, cares, *and* acts."

When the room erupted into applause again, she walked to one side of the stage with outstretched arms.

"The winner today will receive not only a five-thousand-dollar scholarship, but also serious bragging rights." There was scattered laughter around the room. "No, the big prize today isn't the money or the bragging rights, it's the power of these firms backing one single project." She turned to the panel of judges. "This is a group of our industry's most impressive leaders, seven people who have proven to be uniquely gifted at finding the next big thing. Each firm will bring its vast resources to help this one developer take his or her game to the next level. They will spare no expense, right?" she asked. The judges smiled and nodded while the room clapped and cheered.

"Each young developer has six minutes to tell you about his or her game, give you a short demo, and explain why he or she deserves to be this year's Games for Good winner. Are you ready to meet them?"

The music came back on and the nine developers

walked across the stage and stopped in the center. Allie's heart sunk. It was almost impossible to watch. She so desperately wanted to be up there. Her dad must have sensed it, because he reached over and took her hand in his.

Nathan had ditched the shorts and T-shirt, and he was standing with his feet rooted in place, looking confident in dark jeans, a white collared shirt, and a black blazer.

Allie was still so angry with him, but she couldn't help feeling nervous for him, too. After everything they'd been through together that week, she was surprised to realize that she wanted him to win.

"Before we begin, I just have to tell this group how impressed I am with every single developer. I don't get to be a judge, and thank goodness, because I can't imagine picking one of these games. Each has the potential to reach millions, and change the lives of many people. So, on your feet! Be loud and give our developers a big round of applause!"

Everyone stood, clapping and yelling. And then the lights went dark.

Allie could see the shadows of everyone exiting. Then the music and lights came back up, and there was a girl standing in the middle of the stage. The screen behind her was filled with a bright blue water drop and the words WIL'S WAY.

"Thank you, ladies and gentlemen. My name is Lauren Secatero and I'm here today to tell you about Wil's Way, a game designed to bring clean water to developing countries.

This is Wil," she said, pointing proudly to the animated water droplet with big eyes and a wide smile. "Wil stands for Water Is Life, and the name comes from that saying, *Where there's a will, there's a way.*"

She launched her game and Wil bounced along the bottom of the screen. As she tipped her phone up, down, and side to side, the water droplet bounced, climbing a series of platforms and avoiding obstacles like piles of dirt and drains. When Wil reached the empty water glass at the top of the screen, the droplet advanced to the next level. Her game was much simpler than Nathan's, but Allie liked that. At the end of Lauren's presentation, she got a huge round of applause.

After three more presentations, Nathan finally stepped onto the stage. The screen behind him came to life as his little animated characters waddled around his detailed neighborhood with hammers in their hands. Each one took a spot on a ladder next to a tiny house and got to work.

"Last year, I was eleven years old. I was sitting in that seat right there." He pointed to a chair in the front row. "All I could think about was that next year, I wanted to be up here on this stage, demonstrating a game of my own. And here I am. Thank you for letting me introduce you to Built."

Allie couldn't help but think about how much he'd done to get to that point. A year of lunches in the lab. An entire summer in front of his screen. And she found herself clapping along with everyone else.

For the next five minutes, Nathan took the audience on a tour through his town and told them all about his goal to build real houses for people who needed them.

Everyone laughed when he demonstrated his little workers, climbing ladders with hammers in hand. He explained how the store worked on a karma system; each player was encouraged to do kind deeds for a neighbor in exchange for points they could use to buy nails, screws, wood, and paint. In the final minute, he zoomed out so everyone could see the street signs and subtly placed billboards as he told them how sponsorship worked.

"It's simple. For every home that's built, one of our sponsors donates a dollar to Habitat for Humanity. That's it. Just one dollar. Over the last year, I've built more than a thousand of these little houses. I've been the only builder. Obviously." That got a laugh. "If I'd had a sponsor, that would have meant a thousand dollars for Habitat for Humanity. Can you imagine how many real houses we could build if we had twenty or thirty sponsors—each taking turns to donate a dollar—and thousands or even *millions* of players? The more sponsors, the more players, and the smaller the investment but the larger the reward."

He stepped back to the center of the stage. "Thank you for your time and attention. I'm Nathan Fredrickson, creator of Built, and I believe games can change the world."

He ended his presentation with a close-up of the Built icon.

And then Nathan looked down into the first row and locked his eyes on Allie. He gave her the biggest smile and mouthed the words *Thank you*, and she knew he wasn't talking to the judges or the audience. He was talking to her.

There was something about the look on his face—a genuine sincerity mixed with sadness, but not a trace of guilt. She stared at him, and she knew in that moment he hadn't sabotaged her game. He couldn't have. Whatever happened, he hadn't done it on purpose.

Nathan left the stage, and one by one, the final presenters took his place. When the last presentation ended, the music started back up, loud and upbeat, and Naomi Ryan returned to the stage.

"What did I tell you?" She looked over at the judge's desk. "Are you blown away right now?" They all nodded.

"I know we'd all love to see every one of these games succeed out there in the great big world, but raise your hand if there was one game that you found yourself really excited about. One game that spoke to you." Almost every single hand in the room shot into the air.

"In a moment, the judges will choose a winner, and it might not be your favorite. If it's not, here's what you can do about it. Each one has been uploaded on the Spyglass website. Go download it and start playing. Tell your friends. Spread the word. Encourage everyone you know to play these games."

The ten giant screens around the room came to life,

each one showing one of the Games for Good entries. One of the screens stayed fixed on the stage, and Allie wondered if that was where Click'd was supposed to be.

She pushed the thought out of her mind and returned her attention to the other screens. They were all interesting, but she still couldn't take her eyes off Built.

"It looks like we're ready to hear our winner," Naomi Ryan said. She left the stage, and a woman wearing a dark red pantsuit with gray hair and thick black glasses took her place. All the developers returned and stood behind her.

"This was an incredibly difficult decision. The seven of us didn't completely agree. We each had our favorites. But there was one game that had a home on all our top three lists because the design is clean and simple, and the concept is unique and easy to grasp for players of all ages. We chose this game because we felt the cause was timely and its call to action was simple and important."

Allie was perched at the edge of her chair. She looked at Zoe, Maddie, and Emma. All three were sitting on the edges of their seats, too.

"This game is fun," the judge continued. "But it's more than that. It's *addictively* fun."

Allie couldn't stand it. Her heart was pounding so hard she thought it would beat right out of her chest.

"This year's winner of the Games for Good competition is . . ."

Built, Allie thought. *Please say Built.*

"The winner is *Wil's Way!*"

Lauren Secatero threw her hand over her mouth and bent forward like she wasn't sure her knees were going to hold her up. Two of the other girls jumped up and down and hugged her.

"Thank you!" She looked at the judge's table, her eyes glossy with grateful tears. She shook their hands and they congratulated her. "Thank you," she said again.

Allie looked up at Nathan. She could tell he was sad, but he was clapping just as hard and yelling just as loudly as everyone else.

thirty-two

When Allie got back to the Games for Good Pavilion, it was full of people, walking from kiosk to kiosk, meeting each of the developers and watching their demos. Ms. Slade came over several times to check in, and each time she introduced Allie to a bunch of the software executives who had been in the audience.

Eventually, Allie stopped feeling awkward about the fact that she was the only one in the pavilion without a real demo. She got comfortable with her photo slideshow. She told everyone about her friends and their week with Click'd. At first, she only talked about the things that went right, but after a while, she started telling stories about the things that went wrong, too. She even found herself laughing and shaking her head as she explained how "one small, tiny, minuscule change in the code can mess *everything* up and . . ." Then she would let out a long sigh and say, "Anyway, that's what happened to me. But I'll fix it. And I'll relaunch it. And soon, Click'd will be clicking again."

The more she said it, the more she started to believe it.

Occasionally, she'd glance over at Nathan's booth and see him gesturing wildly with his hands like he always did when talking about Built. She felt that pang of guilt again, just like she had when she'd seen him onstage. She could tell he loved his game. He believed in it. He never thought he needed to take her down to win Games for Good.

Like she'd been telling people all day: *She* made a mistake at some point. *She* missed something. *She* broke Click'd.

When all the booth traffic finally slowed down, Allie took a big sip of water and then crouched down, reaching into her backpack and feeling around for her lip gloss. She peeked inside and saw her spiral-bound notebook, and pressed in between its pages, she saw the printout Nathan had given her in the lab on Thursday right before they'd left for the day. She gave it a tug and pulled it out.

She looked over her code, paying special attention to

the commands Nathan had highlighted in blue, and especially to that last line, highlighted in green. That line "was what tied it all back to the leaderboard," he had said. She stared at that line, like she'd stared at it the whole night and most of the day before.

Her booth was still quiet, so she went back to her monitor, moved her presentation into the background, and opened a browser window. She navigated over to the CodeGirls server, opened her code, and found the area she'd changed on Thursday night.

She held Nathan's printout up to the monitor and compared them. She'd deleted the lines of code he'd told her to. And the line he'd highlighted in green matched up perfectly, too.

But then she noticed something strange. Not in Nathan's printout, but in her code on the screen.

In his printout, there was a line after the one he'd told her how to rework. But when she looked at her code, it was missing.

She looked at the piece of paper again. And back at the screen. And then back at Nathan's printout.

After the line of code she rewrote—the one that reworked the way the photos connected to the leaderboard—there was supposed to be another line.

Nathan had included it in his printed instructions. But it wasn't in her code.

She thought back to Thursday night. It was almost

midnight when she made the changes. She hadn't meant to even touch that line of code, but maybe she'd accidentally deleted it. It was late. She was tired. It was possible.

Allie's chest felt heavy.

She'd known in her gut it wasn't Nathan's fault, and now she had proof.

She thought about the look on his face when he first installed her app. She remembered the way he joked with her as he took her quiz, how he made her take his profile picture, and the way he smiled when Click'd put her in the top spot on his leaderboard. She thought about Nathan flipping his phone upside down, saying that one friend was enough for him. And she thought about the way she smiled when he called her Gator.

She retyped the missing line of code exactly the way it was on the printout, and when she was done, she compared the two again. It looked perfect. She held her breath and pressed SAVE. And then she refreshed the data and pressed the UPDATE button without even testing it.

She took out her phone and launched Click'd.

Her profile looked exactly the way it did on the bus the day before, right before it started crashing.

She clicked on the leaderboard and found that it was completely full with her top ten friends on Bus #14.

It was working again.

She couldn't believe her eyes. She opened all the screens, trying to make it crash, but it refused to.

She knew she should probably leave it alone, but she couldn't help herself. She navigated over to her user list. There were flag icons next to thirty-two names; the kids on Bus #14. But she could still see the original list of twelve hundred members, and scrolled down until she found Nathan's information. She clicked on the icon to flag it and reactivate his record.

Bloop-bloop-bloop.

She looked down at her screen and saw an old picture of Nathan, standing between Cory and Mark. She recognized the gym of their elementary school. It was taken during the fifth-grade science fair.

Allie glanced over at Nathan's kiosk. He was surrounded by a big group of people wearing black shirts with the Stardust Games logo on the back. He was talking with them, but she could tell he'd heard the sound, too, because he touched his back pocket and kept stealing glances over at her.

She waved.

After the Stardust executives shook Nathan's hand and walked away, she watched him pull his phone from his pocket. He looked at his screen and smiled. And then he started walking toward her kiosk.

Allie tightened her grip on her phone and started walking toward him.

The picture on her screen was bright red and flashing fast when they met in the middle of the pavilion.

"Hi." Allie smiled nervously.

Nathan smiled back. "Hey. You got it working, huh?"

"Yeah." Allie's heart was racing. Her hands felt clammy and her mouth was dry. She tipped her head toward her kiosk. "I just found your printout in my bag and . . . it looks like I accidentally deleted the line right after the one you told me to change." Allie swallowed hard. "I feel so stupid."

He shook his head. "Don't. It was late at night. It was an easy mistake."

"No, not about that," she said. "About blaming you when you didn't do anything wrong."

It was quiet for a long time. Finally, Nathan said, "I never would have done that to you. You know that, right?"

She pulled in a deep breath. "I know. I'm so sorry."

He looked at her like he was trying to figure out what to say next. "That was horrible," he finally said.

"What was?"

"Seeing you in the audience today. You should have been up there with the rest of us."

"It's okay. You were great up there. And I'm happy for you. I really am."

She held her phone out toward Nathan. He smiled as he tapped his against it. Their screens flashed bright white and their leaderboards appeared.

"Nice to see you back, Gator."

Allie smiled. "You too, Nate."

Click'd

Allie Navarro

Leaderboard

1	Nathan	2	Zoe
3	Hannah	4	Grace
5	Simon	6	Marcus
7	Molly	8	Hallie
9	Rachel	10	Penny

Click'd

Nathan Frederickson

Leaderboard

1	Allie	2	?
3	?	4	?
5	?	6	?
7	?	8	?
9	?	10	?

Then something over Nathan's shoulder caught Allie's attention. There was an even larger group of people in Stardust Games tees at his kiosk that time, and they seemed to be looking for him.

"What's that all about?" she asked, pointing toward them.

Nathan turned around and followed her gaze. "Executives from Stardust. I guess they're all excited about Built. They really liked my presentation."

"That's awesome."

"Remember Rescued, that game for shelter animals from last year?" he asked. Allie remembered it well. She even had the game on her phone. "Well, it didn't win, but Stardust funded it and it now it's a top game on all the online app stores. They want to do the same thing for Built."

"Seriously?"

"They said they'll give me space in their labs and a few additional developers, and they'll handle all the marketing. They think they can help get top corporate sponsors, and with the right backing, they say Built could really take off."

Allie didn't hear much enthusiasm in his voice. "That's good news, isn't it?"

"Well, that depends." He shrugged. "They want to see what they called 'proof-of-concept' first. They said if I can get two thousand downloads by the end of the month, they're in."

"Two thousand? That's nothing! If I can get a thousand users in a week, you can get two thousand users in a month, no problem!"

Nathan laughed. "No, *you* can get two thousand downloads in a month. Built isn't a naturally viral game like Click'd is."

"Well, it should be!" As soon as the words slipped from her mouth, she had an idea. She stopped talking. She could see it forming in her mind. And she knew exactly what she needed to do.

She remembered that day Nathan downloaded her app and asked, *What are you going to do with all this data?*

She didn't have a good answer at the time.

But now she did.

Sunday

thirty-three

"Allie." The voice sounded soft and far away.
"Allie, wake up."

She peeled one eye open. The sun was shining brightly
through the crack in her bedroom curtains, and she let out
a groan as she squeezed her eyes shut again. Her face was
sore and her neck was stiff.

"Did you sleep here?" her dad asked.

"I guess so." She peeled her cheek from the keyboard.

"We have to get going," her dad said. "Your game starts
in an hour."

Allie let her head fall back onto her desk. She'd been up

practically all night. There was no way she could play soccer. "Can I skip it today? Please?"

"Skip it? No way. We haven't seen you play all summer. Besides, you can't let your team and your coach down."

Allie yawned loudly.

"I'm making pancakes. Be downstairs in ten minutes." He left her room and closed the door behind him.

Allie tried to focus her eyes on her computer monitor. She blinked fast, taking in all the lines of code, forcing herself to remember where she'd left off the night before.

Slowly, it all came back to her. She reverted to the original code, and then she made Nathan's changes again, correctly that time. It passed all her tests on the first attempt. She was feeling brave, so she decided to keep going. She wrote a bunch of code to tie the ClickPics back in, and then she tested it again. And it passed.

Somewhere around 3:00 a.m., she broke all her data up by schools and created new groups, separating everyone so there was no crossover between Mercer and Steinbeck. Right before she'd drifted off to sleep, she'd written a screen that required every user to choose an existing group or create a new one.

And she'd written new terms of use. They explained how Click'd randomly pulled photos from Instagram and stored the ClickPics in the photos app, and outlined in clear terms that the information gathered would never be sold, but might be used for research purposes and app recommendations.

She wished she hadn't fallen asleep when she had been so close. Now she looked over everything, feeling good about her progress. She sent the update to her phone and went through every screen, one at a time.

She opened Maddie's profile. Then Zoe's. Then Nathan's. Click'd didn't crash.

She switched from the Mercer group to the CodeGirls group, and her face lit up when she saw the CodeGirls data, back where it was supposed to be. She toggled over to the Mercer group again, back to the CodeGirls group, over to the Steinbeck group, and back to the Mercer group again.

Click'd still didn't crash.

Even though the data had been restored, the leaderboards were still empty. Everyone would have to reclick, but Allie didn't think anyone would mind; that was the fun part. Allie did a little dance in her seat, and Bo walked over and rested his chin on her leg. "I think we're ready," she said to him.

She didn't have time to second-guess anything, and at that point she figured she had nothing to lose. She quickly typed out a message, addressed it to the entire user base, and pressed SEND.

SECURITY UPDATE: REQUIRED INSTALL

And then she changed into her soccer uniform and headed downstairs for breakfast, with Bo leading the way.

thirty-four

As soon as Allie arrived at the fence that lined the soccer field, she spotted Emma stretching along with the rest of the team, and Maddie and Zoe warming up a few feet away.

The second she stepped onto the turf, her phone *blooped*. She smiled, walking faster, heading toward her friends. *Bloop-bloop.*

Now they heard it, too. Maddie and Zoe stopped kicking the ball and ran back to their bags, digging around for their phones.

Zoe found hers first. She held it up in the air, wearing a big smile on her face, and as Allie got closer, the *bloop* sounded three times. A red-tinted photo of Zoe in her soccer uniform and all her goalie gear took over her screen.

"It's back," Zoe said as she jumped in place.

"It's back," Allie said.

They clicked their phones together and watched their phone glow white and their leaderboards come to life.

"Aw, we're ones again," Zoe said, but when Allie didn't respond right away, she knew that wasn't exactly the way it was on Allie's side. "Right? Am I your number one friend?"

For now, Allie thought.

"What's that look on your face?" Zoe asked.

Allie could feel her cheeks getting hot. "Well, I mean we're ones right now, but . . ."

Zoe smirked. "But you'll have a new one when you see Nathan again, huh?"

Allie shrugged and smiled. Then she turned to address the group. "I'm going to need you guys to be my street team again tomorrow."

"Of course," Maddie said.

"No problem," Emma chimed in.

"Sure," Zoe added, "but I'm not sure you need us. Everyone's been missing Click'd."

"Yeah, especially Zoe," Emma said as she slapped her arm with the back of her hand. "Look at her. She's getting all twitchy. She can't wait for this soccer game to be over so she can go play."

Zoe rolled her eyes. "She's right. You guys want to go to the mall later?"

Allie started to tell them all about her plan, but then the air horn sounded and the game began, and they all sprinted to the field and took their positions. And for the next hour, they ran, passed, kicked, and worked together as a team.

When Emma scored the first point, the five of them ran over to her and threw their arms around her shoulders.

At halftime, they all ran to the goal and congratulated Zoe on all the shots she'd blocked.

In the third quarter, Maddie made a killer pass to Allie, but Allie missed it entirely. One of the Ravens stole it and took it all the way to the other end and scored.

Allie ran over to Maddie and dropped her head on her shoulder. "Sorry. I think I'm too exhausted for this." Maddie laughed and promised to keep the ball as far away from her as possible for the rest of the game.

When the Ravens scored again, Emma yelled, "It's all good. We've got this!"

And for a little while, it was as if the last week hadn't even happened. And the four of them just felt like the four of them again.

thirty-five

Allie's friends went to the mall right after the game, but she went straight home and got back to work. For the rest of the afternoon, she closely monitored the data.

By noon, almost three hundred people had installed the update.

At two, more than five hundred had installed it.

At three, there were a bunch of new groups and she had more than one hundred new users. She could tell Maddie, Zoe, and Emma were spreading it around the mall, and she laughed when she saw all the new ClickPics pouring in featuring her friends with complete strangers.

At four, when she was nearing fourteen hundred users, she typed out a text to Nathan.

Allie

> what are you doing right now?

Nathan

nothing why?

> come over? I want to show you something.

Allie texted him her address, and an hour later she heard the doorbell ring. She sprinted down the stairs, but her mom was already in the entryway, opening the front door.

"Hi. I'm Nathan." He sounded nervous. "I'm a friend of Allie's."

Bloop-bloop-bloop.

Her mom pulled the door open wider so he had room to step inside. "Of course!" she said excitedly. "I saw your presentation yesterday. I loved your game! Congratulations."

"Thanks," Nathan said.

Her mom pointed to the kitchen. "I'm making dinner. Would you like to stick around and join us?"

Nathan looked up and saw Allie standing on the bottom step. When she nodded approvingly, he turned back to her mom and said, "Sure."

Suddenly, Bo came racing down the stairs. He flew past Allie and stopped at Nathan's feet. He sat looking up at him, his tail wagging excitedly.

Nathan crouched down. "Hi there!" he said as he reached out with both hands and rubbed Bo's back. "Who's this?"

"This is Bo. The best dog in the world."

Nathan stopped petting him and looked at her. "That's impossible. My dog, Archie, is the best dog in the world."

Allie rolled her eyes. "Are we actually going to compete over who has the best dog?"

"Yep." He covered Bo's ears with his hands. "Because I have the best dog."

"No, you don't."

He raised an eyebrow. "Yes, I do."

She rolled her eyes. Allie and Nathan tapped their phones together, and then Allie curled her finger toward her chest. "Follow me. I have something to show you."

They climbed the stairs and Allie led Nathan into her room. She sat down at her computer and opened all the data stored on the CodeGirls server.

"So . . . something you said yesterday got me thinking. Thanks to Click'd, I have all this data, right?" She scrolled down through the user information. "I have all the basic profile stuff, plus answers to fifty questions from more than fourteen hundred people, and I'm getting more every day. You once asked me what I was going to do with all of it, and I didn't know. It hadn't really occurred to me to analyze it until yesterday, but now that I have, I feel like I have a pretty good understanding about my user base."

Allie had created new check boxes, filters, and a pull-down menu to help her easily sort everything.

"Check it out. These three hundred and sixty-eight people are into charitable causes and do-gooder-type stuff. You can tell because of the way they answered questions four, twelve, nineteen, and forty-three."

She unchecked the CAUSES box and clicked one titled GAMES instead. A new set of names filled the screen. "These four hundred and ninety people love video games. I know this because of the way they answered questions six, twenty-seven, and forty-four."

Allie filtered the data again. "These two hundred and eighty-four users like crafts and making things." She selected another box. "And these three hundred and fifty-eight people like the outdoors and things like extreme sports, which isn't the same as building a house or anything, but I figured it was kinda close."

"Where are you going with this?"

Allie leaned back in her chair. "Did you install the update I sent out this morning?"

"Yeah."

"Three new screens popped up before the install began. Do you remember what they said?"

Nathan thought about it. "There was a user agreement."

"Yep," Allie said.

"And I had to give it permission to access Instagram and photos."

She nodded.

He looked out of the corner of his eye, like he was trying to visualize the third screen. And then he grinned. "It was an opt-in. It asked if I wanted to be notified about similar apps and games."

A huge smile spread across Allie's face. "Did you check the box?"

"Yeah, I think so."

"You did. I know so." Allie turned back toward the monitor. "You agreed. And so did these nine hundred eighty-four users." She sorted the data again and their names filled the monitor. "This is all of them, broken up into four categories based on their specific interests."

"Are you saying what I think you're saying?"

"If you're thinking that we're going to send them the link for Built, then yes." She opened all the categorized user data again. "And we're going to use their interests in video games, crafts, outdoor activities, and causes to craft specific messages to each group."

Nathan stared at the screen for a long time.

"You seem to be at a loss for words," Allie said. He

didn't take his eyes off the screen. Allie wasn't even sure he'd blinked. "That's kind of a new thing for you."

He ran his fingers through his hair. "Why are you doing this for me?" he finally asked.

"I'd do anything for my friends," Allie said with a shrug. "And what can I say? I keep trying to get rid of you, but you just keep coming back. Always in that number one spot."

Monday

thirty-six

Allie rested her lunch tray against one hip and used her free hand to check her jeans pocket. Yep. Her phone was still there. Just like it had been two minutes earlier.

Relax, she told herself. *It's all good.*

As Allie walked to the old oak tree, she looked around the quad. Every once in a while, she'd hear a *bloop* and see two people walk toward each other and quietly tap their phones together, but it wasn't like last week. Most people had already reclicked. Now they were forming new groups like "Mercer + Steinbeck" and planning new leaderboard parties after school at the mall, so they could click with kids in nearby towns.

Mr. Mohr stopped as he passed by her. "Congratulations, Ms. Navarro," he said. "Ms. Slade told me you were brilliant at the Games for Good competition."

"Thank you, Mr. Mohr. But . . . I didn't compete. And I didn't win."

He kept walking. "I know that, too."

Allie smiled to herself and continued to her table. When she arrived, Emma and Zoe scooted over to make room, and she sat down between them. Then she looked across the table at Maddie. And then at Chris, who was sitting next to her. He whispered something in her ear, and Maddie blushed and scooted closer to him.

Allie pressed her hands flat against the table. "Best. Street. Team. Ever."

"It's working?" Maddie asked.

"Perfectly. I've heard people talking about Built in every one of my classes today, and when I saw Nathan before school started this morning, he said his user base skyrocketed overnight."

"Is he out here?" Emma asked, scanning the quad. "I'm dying to show him my neighborhood. I've already built twelve houses and my karma points are going through the roof!" She laughed loudly. "No pun intended."

Allie scanned the quad. Nathan wasn't sitting at any of the tables. He wasn't over on the grass near the parking lot. She glanced behind her. She could see Cory and Mark sitting at one of the tables next to the basketball court, but he wasn't with them, either.

"Oh, there's Ajay," Zoe said. "I'm going to go say hi."

Allie watched her walk away, still trying to figure out why Nathan wasn't out in the quad. He had no reason to be in the lab. But she had a sinking feeling he was. "I'll be right back," she said as she stood, leaving her lunch on the table.

She turned on her heel and started walking through the quad. A bunch of people stopped her along the way.

"It's better than ever," one guy said.

"I'm so glad it's fixed," a girl at another table told her.

"That was the *longest* weekend ever!" another girl said. "Please don't let that happen again." She laughed and gave Allie a high five.

"I won't," Allie said.

Then Allie felt a tap on her shoulder. She turned around and found Claire Friedman standing there, bouncing in place. "I'm so glad you're my seven again! And I love the new groups feature. Very cool."

"Thanks," Allie said.

"Do you want to sit with us?" she asked as she pointed over at her table. "My friends are dying to meet you."

But Allie gestured in the opposite direction. "Maybe another time. I need to find someone."

Claire took off, and Allie continued on. As grateful as she was to have so many happy users, she knew there were plenty of unhappy former users, too. Tucked into her backpack, she had a printed list of everyone who had downloaded and deleted Click'd, and she was on a personal mission to find each one and apologize before the week was over.

Allie opened the door to the computer lab. She hoped she wouldn't see Nathan there, but she spotted him right away, hanging out with Agnes. He had his headphones over his ears, head-bobbing in time with the music.

She fell into the seat next to him, and he wrapped his headphones around the back of his neck.

"What are you doing in here?" she asked.

"Watching," he said as he pointed at his monitor. Allie scooted her chair closer. He had a bird's-eye view of the whole game. He could see all the players running around the neighborhood with their avatar names in little bubbles above their heads. There were hundreds of them.

"These aren't test characters." He tapped his finger on the glass. "Real, actual people are making them move and build and buy things." He turned to her. "There are real people playing my game. Can you believe that?"

"Yeah, I can totally believe that."

"And look at this." Nathan switched screens and his browser filled with news stories he'd collected from a Google search. She read the headlines.

Playing for Good
Teens Change the Game
What a Difference a Game Makes

"These articles have been coming in all day, and every single one includes screenshots and the download link for Built."

He opened an article that included a photo of the developers onstage, side by side, and Allie felt another pang of sadness. She wished so badly that she could have been up there with them. If she'd only let Nathan help her back in the lab on Friday, he might have noticed her mistake. The two of them might have had it fixed by lunchtime. She might have been in that picture.

But there was no sense thinking about it now.

Nathan seemed to read her mind, or maybe he caught the expression on her face, because he closed the window quickly and said, "I'm so sorry. I don't know what I was thinking."

Allie shook it off. "It's okay. Really." She tipped her chin toward the monitor. "How many downloads?"

Nathan switched back to his game and pointed to the number in the corner. "Seven hundred sixty-four."

The two of them sat there for a few minutes, watching his screen, completely mesmerized by a group of players gathered around one house, working together to paint it bright blue.

"Hey," Allie said. "I know you're thrilled that real people are playing Built, but do you know where else there are real people?" She tipped her head toward the door. "Outside. In the quad. There's also this thing called sun."

She formed a circle with her hands. "Big yellow thing. Hangs out in the sky during the day. Perhaps you've heard of it?"

Nathan kicked his heels up on the desk, crossed one ankle over the other, and leaned back against the wall. "Eh . . . sun, shmun. I like it in here. It's quiet. And we have snacks." He reached for his bag of microwave popcorn and stuffed a handful into his mouth.

Allie took the bag away and set it on her side of the table, out of his reach.

"You need to get out of here, Nathan. Go to the quad. Find your friends. Trust me on this." She gestured toward the door again.

He shook his head. "No thanks."

Allie leaned in closer. "Why not?"

He didn't say anything for almost a full minute. And then he shrugged. "I don't even know where I'd go."

Allie felt like her heart might break into a million little pieces.

"I saw Cory and Mark on my way here. They're down on the blacktop, sitting at a table next to the basketball courts."

He forced a laugh. "And what am I supposed to do, sit down and join them?"

"Yeah. Why not?"

"Because I've barely talked to them in over a year. We say hi in the halls and stuff, but it's not like I can sit down and start chatting like we're all old friends."

"But you *are* old friends. You've known them all your life. You'll see. Once you sit down it will be easy. Maybe you'll *bloop* and Click'd will break the ice. And if you don't, just ask them about their weekends. Tell them about yours. Show them your game, tell them about the competition, and talk about all your new users and the news coverage you're getting today. You're famous! You're like Zayn, but better. You're *Naaaate*." She drew out the name and he turned toward her and smiled.

"You make it sound easy," he said.

"It will be. I promise." Allie rested her elbows on her knees and leaned in closer to him. "Come on. I'll help you."

Nathan sighed as he took off his headphones and dropped them on his desk. "Fine."

He followed Allie out of the lab and into the hallway. They walked in silence until they reached the quad, and then they stood under the awning in the shade, scanning the scene. Allie spotted Cory and Mark, still at the same table on the blacktop.

"See, they're right down there," she said, but when she looked over at Nathan, all the color seemed to have drained from his face, making him look like he had twice as many freckles as usual.

"Lunch is almost over now. I'll go up to them tomorrow." He started to walk away, but Allie grabbed his arm.

"There's still fifteen minutes." She wasn't about to let him off the hook that easily. "Nate." He locked his eyes on her. "You can do this."

"I'm ridiculously nervous." He held his hand out in front of him, and she could see it trembling.

Allie rested her hand on the back of his. She wrapped her fingers around it.

"On the count of three," she said.

He drew in a breath. "One."

"Two."

"Three," he said, and she dropped his hand.

"Go."

She watched him walk across the quad and down the steps that led to the blacktop. He ran his hand through his hair a few times and adjusted his T-shirt. At one point, he stopped, and she wondered if he was going to turn around and chicken out. But he kept walking.

When he got close enough, he stopped. He said something, and Cory and Mark turned around. They smiled. And then they scooted over to make room between them.

acknowledgments

Some dads teach their kids how to build a car; mine taught me how to build a computer. Back in Silicon Valley in the early '80s, my dad oversaw and often worked on assembly lines, manually building the very first PCs. He often brought his work home with him, and when he did, I got to help (and make a little extra money). We'd spend hours out in the garage at night and on weekends, where he taught me how to crimp wires, solder them to the motherboard, and then test each connection to be sure it passed quality control. It wasn't easy. My hands hurt after a while. And it was beyond frustrating when a component would fail and I'd have to take it apart and start all over. But honestly . . . I loved the work. And when he gave me a brand-new IBM 5150 and told me *I'd* built it, I was bursting with pride. So, thank you, Dad, for putting a soldering iron in your eleven-year-old daughter's hands. You not only taught me how to build things, you taught me how to fail. And how to start over. And how to keep going until I eventually got it right.

I've wanted to write a book that celebrated my inner geek for so many years! In addition to my dad, I need to thank a few other important geeks in my life, like Ed Niehaus, who gave me my first job in public relations and taught me how to merge my love of writing with my love for all things tech-y. Thanks to Molly Davis and Stacy Peña, two of the smartest people I've ever met, for going on a great big adventure with me to start a business all our own. Every single day, I'm proud of what we built together. And to Mike, my very favorite geek in the whole world. We never would have met if it weren't for our shared fascination with the tech world, so for all the amazing and life-changing experiences this industry has given me, I'm most thankful that it gave me the love of my life.

My kids inspire all my stories, but I see them in the pages of this one more than any of the others. I'd describe Allie and Nathan as strong, determined, bighearted, big-thinking, funny, and most importantly, kind. It's no coincidence that I'd use those same words to describe my kids. Aidan and Lauren: Thank you for being exactly who you are. I love every little thing about you.

I've had a blast writing this book, and that's largely because I got to work with a bunch of wise and wonderful people throughout the process. Huge thanks and barrels of popcorn to everyone at Disney Hyperion, especially Julie Rosenberg, for her brilliant insights, clear guidance, and superhuman patience; Hannah Allaman, for her many ideas that made this book much better; and to Emily Meehan, for her unwavering support and enthusiasm every step of the way. I'm not sure how I got so lucky to work with the three of you, but I never take it for granted.

The graphics throughout this book made it especially tricky to copyedit, but Mark Amundsen, Rebecca Behrens, Dan Kaufman, and Guy Cunningham paid close attention to every single detail. Thank you for caring about the big and little things.

Everyone on the marketing team is sharp, kind, and so much fun to work with. Thank you to Elke Villa, Holly Nagel, Maggie Penn, Sadie Hillier, and Andrew Sansone for all you do. Special thanks to Dina Sherman, who so passionately shares my novels with teachers and librarians—and thanks to those teachers and librarians who, in turn, so passionately share them with readers. You're all rock stars.

I'm so grateful to my hardworking publicists Seale Ballenger and Cassie McGinty, for shouting from the rooftops about *Click'd*, and to Phil Caminiti for designing this super-fun cover that makes me smile every time I see it.

Now that my agent, Caryn Wiseman, and I have been together for six years and five books, I can say with absolute certainty that I couldn't possibly do this work without her. I'm grateful for all she does, and so proud to be part of the Andrea Brown Literary Agency family.

And last but never least, special thanks to my young readers. Every time I meet you online or in the real world, you impress and inspire me. It's an absolute privilege to write for you. Thank you for reading my stories.

Turn the page to try out some
fun coding activities from

Code.org!

BINARY BRACELETS

INTRODUCTION

Wires carry information through computers in the form of electricity. Most computers communicate information using a set of two options, like "on" and "off," or "positive" and "negative." This is called a "binary" language. Everything a computer does is represented through a set of information coded in binary. In this activity, you can use two colors of beads to represent your name using the Binary Decoder Key included below.

MATERIALS

- Thread
- Two colors of seed beads
  (enough to use eight for each letter of your name)

DIRECTIONS

1. Sort your beads by color.
2. Choose one color to represent the black squares (off) and one color to represent the white squares (on) in the Binary Decoder Key.
3. Find the first letter of your first name in the key and follow the pattern by putting the beads on the thread in the order shown on the key, while pinching one end of the thread to keep the beads in place.

A	■□■■	■■■□	N	■□■■	□□□■
B	■□■■	■■□■	O	■□■■	□□□□
C	■□■■	■■□□	P	■□■□	■■■■
D	■□■■	■□■■	Q	■□■□	■■■□
E	■□■■	■□■□	R	■□■□	■■□■
F	■□■■	■□□■	S	■□■□	■■□□
G	■□■■	■□□□	T	■□■□	■□■■
H	■□■■	□■■■	U	■□■□	■□■□
I	■□■■	□■■□	V	■□■□	■□□■
J	■□■■	□■□■	W	■□■□	■□□□
K	■□■■	□■□□	X	■□■□	□■■■
L	■□■■	□□■■	Y	■□■□	□■■□
M	■□■■	□□■□	Z	■□■□	□■□■

4. Repeat step three until you've spelled out your entire name in binary.

5. Tie both ends of the thread together to keep the beads on your binary bracelet in place.

You've just learned how to store your name to your wrist, just like a computer stores information to its drives! If you'd like, you can make bracelets or necklaces featuring any word or phrase.

This activity is adapted with permission from a lesson by Code.org that is licensed under a Creative Commons Attribution-NonCommercial-ShareAlike 4.0 International License. The original version can be found here: https://code.org/curriculum/course2/14/Teacher

DICE RACE GAME

INTRODUCTION

An algorithm is a list of steps that you can follow to finish a task. Computers need algorithms and programs to show them how to do even simple things that we can do without thinking about them. Because of that, it can be challenging to describe something that comes naturally to you in enough detail for a computer to replicate. To begin to understand how that's done, you can use algorithms to help describe things that people do every day. In this two-person activity, you can create an algorithm to describe how to play the Dice Race Game.

MATERIALS

- Dice
- Pens or pencils
- Paper

DIRECTIONS

1. Copy the below diagram onto a sheet of paper. Leave enough room at the bottom to write your own algorithm.

Game 1	Turn 1	Turn 2	Turn 3	Total	
Player 1	___	___	___	___	Circle the winner
Player 2	___	___	___	___	

Game 2	Turn 1	Turn 2	Turn 3	Total	
Player 1	_____	_____	_____	_____	} Circle the Winner
Player 2	_____	_____	_____	_____	

2. Both players start the game with no points. They each take turns rolling the dice and recording the total of their roll, adding the new number to their old score each turn. The highest score after three turns wins!

3. Play a couple rounds of the Dice Race game. As you're playing, think about how you would describe everything you're doing. What would it look like from the computer's point of view?

4. Once you're done playing, write down your own algorithm for how a computer might run the game and compare it with your partner's algorithm. How are they similar, and how are they different? Work together to create one algorithm that you and your partner think best describes the Dice Race.

This activity is adapted with permission from a lesson by Code.org that is licensed under a Creative Commons Attribution-NonCommercial-ShareAlike 4.0 International License. The original version can be found here: https://code.org/curriculum/course3/10/Teacher

For more lessons, activities, and information about coding, visit Code.org.

Turn the page for a
sneak peek at the sequel to

Click'd

sunday

one

Attention, teen coders!
Want to spend your summer at Spyglass Games?

We're looking for students in grades 6–12 to help create the company's first teen hackathon!

Hackathons are "hacking marathons" that pit team against team in a weekend-long, beat-the-clock coding competition. Work together to create a game, mobile app, or even a robot—in just two days, totally from scratch—and you could win big cash (and big-time bragging rights)!

But first, we need your help creating the perfect summer program. As part of our exclusive development team, you'll take part in your choice of three hackathon weekends, all held on our beautiful San Francisco campus, where you'll share ideas and feedback that will help shape the Spyglass Teen Hackathon for years to come. Come take part in this truly unique, once-in-a-lifetime opportunity! Applicants must have at least two years of coding experience and demonstrate the ability to work quickly and collaboratively. Space is extremely limited. Good luck!

Allie leaned back against her headboard and adjusted the laptop in front of her. She scanned her application one more time to be sure she hadn't missed anything.

Current Grade: 7
Coding Experience: 3 years, Games for Good Finalist
Most Recent Project (include link to demo): Click'd

Click'd. She loved her game, but she wished she had something more recent to share with the selection committee. Something they hadn't already seen. Something they hadn't already seen bomb so spectacularly.

She scrolled down to her essay and read it out loud. It sounded pretty good.

"What do you think, Bo?" Her dog opened one eye when he heard his name, but then closed it again. He snuggled in closer to her hip and tipped his head back so Allie could rub that spot under his chin.

"You're right. I should just send it."

The application wasn't due until the end of the month, but she'd been working on it for weeks. Her mom and dad had both read her essay countless times, and so had her computer science teacher, Ms. Slade. There was no reason to wait. Nothing was going to change before it was due anyway.

She listened to the rain plinking against her bedroom window while her finger hovered over the SUBMIT button.

She was about to click it, when her phone chirped. Bo jumped so high, his body practically left the bed.

She laughed as she reached for the phone and read the text.

Courtney

Good day/bad day?

Allie and Courtney usually did good day/bad day right before they fell asleep at night, just like they used to when they were roommates at CodeGirls Camp the previous summer. But they'd been missing each other more than usual lately, and they seemed to be starting the routine earlier.

Allie

Scored a goal in soccer game today
Went to a movie with my friends
Spyglass sent me passes to Game On

She was waiting for Courtney to respond when the familiar FaceTime ring echoed in the room.

"You're going to Game On Con?" Courtney stared at Allie wide-eyed. Her hair was piled on top of her head in a messy bun, and she was wearing her favorite SUNDAY FUNDAY T-shirt.

Allie sat up straighter. "Um . . . Yeah."

"Game On Con. *The* Game On Con?"

"I'm pretty sure there's only one of them." Spyglass Games held it every January and people came from all over the world to attend, making downtown San Francisco heaven-on-earth for the gaming community. "Because of Click'd, I get to go for free and check out all the new games and stuff."

Allie wasn't about to tell her about the personal meet-and-greet with the CEO, Naomi Ryan. Or how she'd planned to use that time to try to land a spot in the summer hackathon program. Courtney couldn't know about Hackathon. Not yet.

"Nathan's going, too," she said.

Nathan got an even sweeter deal than Allie had. He'd been invited to be onstage during Naomi Ryan's keynote and attend some swanky dinner thing with the development team.

"But you don't even play video games!"

"Sure I do."

Courtney let out a huff. "Name one game you play."

Allie thought about it. She had an old Nintendo DS around her room somewhere, but she hadn't turned it on in years. Besides, she knew that wouldn't count. Courtney was talking about real games, like the ones she played every day after school with her online friends.

Courtney didn't give Allie time to reply. "You're so

lucky. Stuff like this happens right in your *backyard*, all the time. Nothing cool ever happens in Phoenix."

"You have more sun," Allie tried.

"Ha! You can have it. I mean, come on . . . it's January. Right now, it's snowing in half the country, but it's seventy-five degrees here. *Seventy-five degrees*, Allie. That's just not natural!"

Courtney had one of those loud, contagious laughs. Hearing her now reminded Allie of those days in the computer lab over the summer. Courtney's giggle would turn into a full-on belly laugh, and that would make Allie laugh, and then Maya would hear them, and she'd start laughing. That would trigger Kaiya and Li at the next station, and soon everyone in the Fishbowl would be wiping their eyes and trying to catch their breaths, and no one but Courtney and Allie would even know what was so funny in the first place.

"Well, it's been raining for four days straight here in San Francisco," Allie said. "So if you need a break from all that horrible sunshine, you can always come here."

Courtney flopped back onto her bed and lifted the phone high in the air. "Don't tempt me. I'd be there in a heartbeat. And I'll gladly take one of those Game On tickets off your hands."

And then they both got quiet. Courtney stared up at Allie's face on her screen. Allie stared back at Courtney.

"Actually . . ." Allie said slowly, watching the idea start

coming to life in her mind. "They *did* tell me to give my extra pass to a friend."

Courtney rested her hand on her chest. "Last time I checked, *I* was your friend."

"You are most *definitely* my friend." Allie threw her feet to the floor and tapped her toes on her carpet. "Come visit me for the weekend!"

"Really?"

"Sure! We'll go to Game On and then I can spend the rest of the weekend showing you San Francisco! We'll walk across the Golden Gate Bridge, and visit Alcatraz, and go to the top of Coit Tower. We'll do all the things we couldn't do when you were here for camp last summer."

Allie's parents would be so excited. They loved acting like tourists in their own city.

"We'll get hot chocolate at my favorite place in North Beach," Allie continued. "And you can meet Maddie, Emma, and Zoe—they are *so* tired of hearing me talk about you—and you can finally meet Nathan!"

Courtney was on her feet now. She must have been dancing around her room because all Allie could see were bookshelves, her desk, her bed, and her window, all blurring by.

"Allie!" Courtney stopped moving. "That's only two weeks away!"

"Well, today is Sunday, and you'd have to get here on a Friday, so technically it's only twelve days from now."

"Twelve days!" Courtney yelled.

"Twelve sleeps!" Allie added.

Allie pictured Courtney walking through the airport security gates, beaming at her from the top of the escalator. She couldn't wait to throw her arms around Courtney's neck and pull her into the tightest hug she'd ever given her.

"Will your parents say yes?" Courtney asked.

"Sure! I mean, I think so! The conference is free, and you're only one state away . . . the flight couldn't be *that* expensive. And they know how much I miss you!" Allie was talking so fast she had to stop to catch her breath. "Your parents will say yes, too, right?"

"Of course they will!"

Allie ran to her desk and sat down in her chair. She propped the phone up next to her keyboard and opened a browser to one of the online ticketing services. She entered the data into the empty fields:

From: Phoenix
To: San Francisco

Allie hit ENTER. The icon spun in place as the system told her it was searching for the lowest price. Courtney flopped down in her denim beanbag chair, chewing nervously on her fingernail while she waited. Times and flight numbers began filling the screen. There was a celebratory sound as the "fabulous fare" landed at the top.

Allie gulped. She stared in disbelief for a long moment. And then she angled her phone so Courtney could see the screen.

"Four *hundred* dollars! Seriously?"

"Seriously," Allie said.

"How could it be four hundred dollars? It's, like, a two-hour flight. Search it again."

Allie searched it again. Same spinning icon. Same "fabulous fare." Same lump in her throat.

They'd been so excited about it being less than two weeks away, but that was the problem. Allie searched dates further into the future, and sure enough, those tickets were half the price.

"It's too soon." Allie fell back in her chair, feeling totally deflated.

"Do you have any money?" Courtney asked.

Allie shook her head. "None. I spent it all on Christmas presents."

"Same here. I found five bucks in my backpack the other day, but that's all I've got."

"Maybe our parents will split it?"

Courtney laughed again, but this time, there was nothing funny or contagious about it. "Yeah, right."

"It can't hurt to ask," Allie said. "I'll tell them I'll do extra jobs. I'll mow the lawn and give Bo a bath."

"I'll wash the car and babysit my little brother for free," Courtney said.

"They have to say yes."

Courtney got serious again. "I have to go to Game On, Allie. I need to get out of here. I need rain, and you, and thousands of nerdy gamers like me, and—"

"Allie! Dinner!" her mom called from the bottom of the stairs.

Bo knew that word. He ran straight for her bedroom door and sat there, tail wagging, waiting for Allie to open it, so he could follow the smells that led to the kitchen.

"Wish me luck." Allie gave the phone screen a fist bump.

"Luck," Courtney said, bumping her back.